Until Theft Do Us Part

A FOLKLORE FALLS ROMANCE RETELLING

EMILY FLUKE

Also by Emily Fluke

Folklore Falls Romance Retellings

-Until Theft Do Us Part

-Fake Dating's a Beast (releasing October 11th, 2022)

...and more.

The Mari Fable Mysteries

-Death of a Fairy Tale

-Kidnapping the Classics

-The Pinocchio Project (releasing July 5, 2022)

-A Grimm Haunting (releasing December 5, 2022)

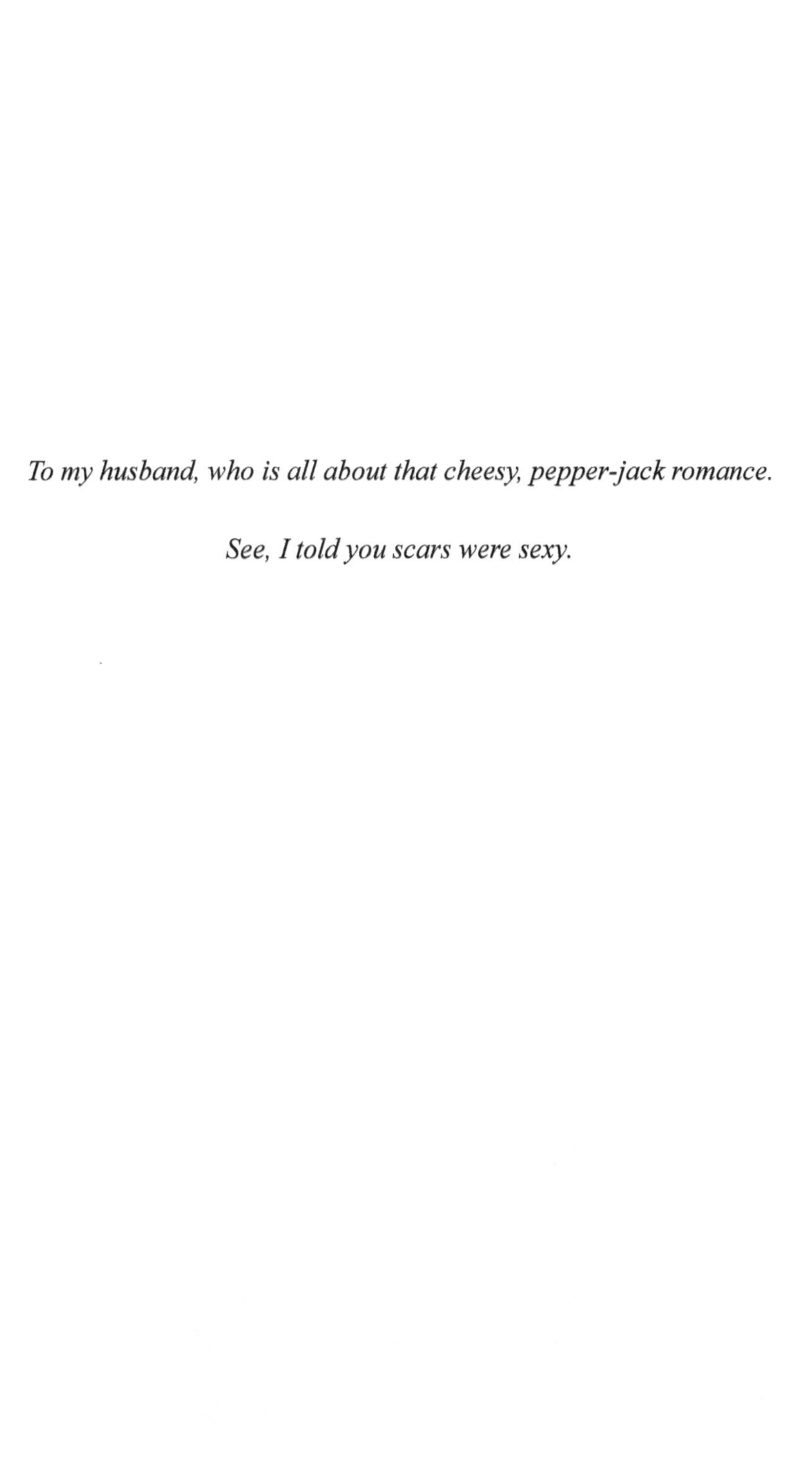

To my husband, who is all about that cheesy, pepper-jack romance.

See, I told you scars were sexy.

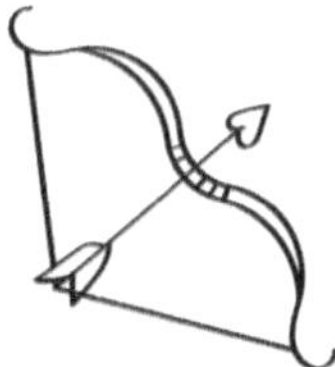

Stealing was like wearing leggings. Some people judged me for it, while others could see right through the fabric of society and know that what I did benefited those who needed it. Of course, in this case, the comfort of the leggings only benefited me.

But I didn't steal the ring, not yet. I slipped a guest's engagement ring into my pocket after replacing it with one of the many I'd borrowed from the pawnshop. It was not necessary for the chick with the manicure that cost more than our bed-and-breakfast rent, but to the widow who lost her husband the same month the tourist resort shut down her bakery, the two-carat diamond would save Diana's house from foreclosure.

I patted my powdered sugar-coated fingers on the black leggings and pressed the fake ring into the soft center of the cake. White hand-prints covered my thighs like crime scene powder used to dust for fingerprints. I was no stranger to criminal activity, but despite my urge to slap those like the heiress about to get engaged in our bed-and-breakfast's quaint dining nook, I'd never hurt a fly. Did I steal from them and maybe suffer a bit of guilt? Yes. But I'd brush the icky feeling away like I did the sugar on my hands.

I plucked the real ring from the pocket in my apron and scrutinized it in the kitchen light. It was princess-cut style, simple, but with a massive diamond and impressive clarity. The ring I'd taken from Johnny's pawnshop that morning matched the popular style. Both pieces of jewelry looked out of place in a kitchen of dirty mixing bowls, a sink full of old-fashioned dishes, and my messy reflection staring back at me from the microwave window.

After I slipped the ring onto my finger and admired it, a thick lump gathered in my throat. My ex had never offered me one of these, and I wouldn't have accepted if he did. I kept too many secrets for a relationship to work, which meant love, marriage, and the whole picket-fence bit didn't fit into my future. But this ring fit perfectly.

Until I tried to take it off.

The white gold dug into my skin as I tugged and yanked.

"Son of a biscuit with gravy," I muttered. The engagement ring clamped around my finger with impossible force. Panic sent my heart thumping.

It wasn't coming off.

Finally, it slipped over my knuckle after carefully wiggling. I could breathe again. This didn't suit me. The only diamonds I cared for were the ones in the lost dagger from the Folklore Falls legend. It kept the history of our town alive. Plus, this ring would help our widowed neighbor survive. I couldn't bring her husband back to life, but I could take this ring and help Diana keep the home she'd shared with him. A diamond this big would pawn for a year's worth of her lost salary.

The kitchen doors swung open and snapped me from my daydream.

"Hey," I said. As quickly as I could, I dropped the stolen ring back into my apron pocket and patted the fabric down.

My mother raised a thin eyebrow as she marched toward me. She was an exact twenty-year-older version of me, with auburn locks twisted into a messy hair claw and eyes that only looked green in the sun. Except her beauty tripled with the enormous heart that exuded with her every smile, soft eyes, and hopelessly romantic outlook on life.

"Loxley," Mama said, as she wiped her hand on her apron, then snapped her fingers in front of my face. She'd only cleaned off some of the flour from the morning's fresh bread and the snap sent white dust floating over my nose until I sneezed. "Earth to Loxley. Mr. Culp is sweating bullets out there while he waits." She waved in the general direction of the dining room. "Get the coffee cake on the table before he blames our staff for his botched proposal. We can't survive another one-star review."

The usual brightness in her voice dipped with the last sentence. My mother worked her booty off for those reviews, especially since the ratings drew vacationers to the quaintness of Sherwood Bed and Breakfast over the massive resort that had landed in Folklore Falls last summer. We couldn't compete with Jensen Resort's heated pools, the view of the falls, and California king-sized beds. The stars we earned came from smiles, delicious homemade waffles, and personal experiences, like the entire Sherwood staff catering to this one rich dude's cheesy-ass proposal.

"Sorry, Mama," I said. I pulled my hand from the pocket of my apron where the heavy diamond weighed down the thin muslin. Even our aprons looked quaint, since I'd spent hours with Grandpa Owl sewing and hand-stitching Sherwood's tree logo and name on the front.

I sprinkled cinnamon sugar over the top of the coffee cake. The dusting of sugar and spice covered the hole where I'd pushed the ring into the spongy deliciousness. I scooped up the plate and followed Mama.

The sweet, nutty scent of waffles wafted from the direction of my mother as she pushed through the kitchen doors. Balancing an excessively large cinnamon streusel cake in my palm, I slipped through before the doors swung shut.

Round tables were spread throughout the dining room in an organized maze I knew better than the scars on my hand. More than half of Sherwood's rooms were filled this weekend because a rich guy had flown his girlfriend's whole family to our small town for the proposal. It was good to see the bed-and-breakfast almost full, but I tried not to think of how bare it would look this summer when fancy vacationers arrived and selected Jensen Resort over the hometown experience our inn offered.

But we catered to proposals, honeymoons, and even weddings with more personality. Sherwood Bed and Breakfast dripped with romance. It was disgusting. But I put on a beaming smile as fake as the ring in the center of the cake.

Beads of sweat lined the guy's forehead and shined in the morning sun that streamed in through the big bay windows. It looked like a beacon calling my attention to their table. When he turned to glance at me and the coming engagement ring, his shaggy hair flopped into his face. If he didn't wear a shirt that cost more than a year's worth of my college tuition, he might be attractive. But wavy locks or not, I'd never find myself interested in a man who'd been born with a silver spoon in his mouth. Rich people based their entire personalities on material possessions and name brands. They bored me to tears.

I maneuvered through the crowded room of chairs and bodies with practiced ease and stopped in front of the couple's table. A smudge on the window behind the girlfriend's head made me cringe, but I kept the smile plastered on my face. I took pride in the cleanliness of our B and B and the presentation of our staff since I could never get myself together. I swiped a lock of hair from my face and wished I'd asked someone dressed nicer to deliver the cake with the ring, but I didn't want to risk getting someone else in trouble for the swap.

Mr. Culp thanked me for the breakfast cake, and I slipped from the scene before he dropped to one knee. Mama and I stood by the kitchen doors to watch as the girlfriend dipped her fork into the cake and the metal prongs clinked against the ring.

Mama clutched my bicep and let out a tiny squeak as we witnessed the guy scoot to the edge of his seat and bend down on his knee in front of the table. I rolled my eyes. This theft was so easy I almost felt guilty. In fact, I only stole from those who blatantly didn't care for others, and this guy gave me an all-access pass when he'd thrown his car keys and hit Grandpa Owl in the face. Grandpa Owl told him we didn't offer valet, but the guy still refused to park his own Bentley. Hell, our resident nocturnal seamster couldn't see well enough to drive during the day, much less at night. Good thing I'd just come back from a run of pickpocketing the snobs at Jensen Resort when the Bentley owner demanded Grandpa Owl's service.

I'd considered driving off with the car when I took it around the back of Sherwood's building, but grand theft auto wasn't my style. I moved in the shadows like the fox that kept snatching our baby chicks from the coop. The desire to avoid getting caught was almost as strong as my need to stay anonymous. Folklore Falls residents didn't take well to charity. They were a hard-working stock of humans. But when Jensen Resort drove their businesses into the ground this past year, they'd needed to pocket their pride and accept some help. Anonymous donations eased that pain.

The girlfriend's squeal snapped me back to the present. The fake jewel caught the glint of sunlight but only sent a single, rugged glow darting around the ceiling rather than hundreds of shining reflections like a genuine diamond.

I patted the small lump in the apron's pocket and assured myself it'd help the widowed baker before her unpaid mortgage sent her house into foreclosure.

As I watched the couple, a small twinge tickled the spot between my stomach and rib cage where I'd suffered heartburn this past year. Grandpa Owl liked to remind me I'd aged. But making it past my mid-twenties didn't denote spinster status. I didn't blame the old seamster for pushing me to marry young since he'd lost the love of his life to cancer before they'd made it down the aisle.

The story almost convinced me to date again, but I'd never figured out how to explain my nightly disappearances to a significant other. Eventually, a boyfriend would find out about my breaking and entering, thievery, and unhealthy obsessions with the archery range and sour beer. While I could lie better than a hen with an egg, I didn't want a relationship based on dishonesty.

The girlfriend—now fiancée—grinned as her man slipped the fake ring onto her finger. The roomful of their family erupted into cheers. I clapped as an automatic response, always the good hostess.

A quick glance at Mama told me her glee was genuine, and I admired her honesty. Someday, when the town didn't need the financial support my spoils provided, I'd be like her; innocent and honorable. Mama's misty eyes sent my heart to my stomach, and it seemed my pulse beat right behind the apron, bumping the bulge in the pocket with an erratic rhythm. She only wanted the best for her guests, rude snobs or not, and she was a sucker for cheesy displays of love—something that my father refused to give her when they were still together.

Mr. Culp's father snapped his fingers in the air for attention.

"Hey, you," he shouted and pointed at Mama. When she hurried over to him, I pricked my ears to focus on their conversation over the oohs and ahhs that surrounded the brand-new fiancée.

"Our sausages were too greasy," he said with a flick of his head toward the empty plate from his breakfast. "Could we get a refund?"

While Mama offered him an extra meal for free, I pictured myself slapping the guy in the face with a sausage and then asking him what he thought of the grease after that. Now I knew where the son had learned his awful behavior. But if the apple always fell that close to the tree, I wouldn't be a thief.

I snorted and shook my head at that thought. Before I turned to disappear back into the kitchen, the couple's public display of affection caught my eye.

They paused just before a kiss, and the man whispered something to his fiancée. Her gaze flicked from his lips to his eyes, then back to his lips. Though chaos surrounded them, and their family demanded attention, pictures, and speeches, they looked to be inside their own bubble of love.

My heart skipped a beat as the man's hand trailed up his fiancée's arm and then landed behind her ear. I bit my lip as theirs pressed together in a gentle yet intimate kiss. It had been exactly twenty-seven thefts since I'd experienced a moment like that. And that was only because my ex had come back into town, and I'd stooped low enough to let Mama convince me I was lonely. Mine and my ex's kiss definitely hadn't come with the love that this couple shared.

When the woman pulled away, she stretched her arm out and admired the engagement ring. I zoned out and stared at them while trying to avoid thoughts about the warmth of another person's arms around me. The delicious smell of maple syrup drifted from the kitchen, but it didn't lift my spirits as much as usual. Warm waffles filled my belly every day, but the other pillow on my bed stayed cold since I'd sworn off dating.

The woman's smile twisted into a frown, and she pulled her hand closer to her face. Her mouth dropped open, and she slipped the ring off to show it to her man.

I caught bits of her words between the dozens of conversations buzzing in the room. My lips parted as I held my breath.

"This isn't real," she said with a quivering voice. I'd heard those words many times before from vacationers just like them who claimed the legend of Folklore Falls wasn't history.

Mr. Culp yanked it from her hand and pinched his brows. He angled it toward the window to catch the sunshine, but it didn't shine the way her earrings did.

A lump gathered in my throat as I tried to step back and push through the kitchen doors. But before my feet could move, the guy's sharp gaze went from the knockoff ring and straight to me.

Uh oh.

Maybe this theft wasn't as easy as I'd thought.

Two

The thin fabric of my leggings didn't protect my legs from rug burn. After dropping to my knees, I scooped up the pawned ring that Mr. Culp had chucked on the floor as if he was allergic to anything less than half a million dollar jewelry.

"Where did the fake ring come from?" he shouted, spittle splashing over Mama's face. I curled my lip and narrowed my eyes at him.

Mr. Culp fumed and bared his teeth like a grizzly before spouting another string of threats that included having my mother arrested, buying out the B and B then bulldozing it, and assuming Sherwood staff's low education level because people like him viewed people like us as stupid.

Money has nothing to do with intelligence. Which is clear by the fact that you bought a diamond from a company that's notorious for violence and corruption. That was what I wanted to say.

"It's my fault." That was what I really said. I didn't want to give the expensive piece of jewelry back—not after what the future Mrs. Culp's company had done to Diana and her husband, but I didn't want to waste Sherwood staff's time and energy, either. Her company had paid our neighbor's husband pennies while the future Mrs. Culp drank exorbitant amounts of champagne funded by the money she'd saved by withholding benefits and raises.

"Incompetent—" Mr. Culp interrupted himself with a scoff and rubbed his palm over his face. He sighed and struck a finger at me. "You're going to pay for this."

"Two wrongs don't make a right," Mama said, trying to calm him. It was her favorite phrase. One that pricked my conscience every time. This time, she repeated it to the Culp family with an apology after Mr. Culp threatened to shut down Sherwood Bed and Breakfast. Her gentle voice and sweet smile calmed him, despite the sneaky suggestion in her phrase. *Please don't attack us for this mistake.*

I shuffled a step back and fidgeted like I was nervous and toying with the apron. I let the ring fall out of my apron right behind Mama's foot. When she stepped back, she'd find it, return it to Mr. Evil and be the heroine of the day. Less than half of what she deserved.

I stood and silently cursed at myself for letting my poor Mama take the blame. I never wanted to involve her in this but I'd acted impulsively when I'd taken the Culps' engagement ring.

It was only a day ago that I'd learned the future Mrs. Culp was related to the company that screwed over our neighbor's husband. My anger and skill with stealing pushed me to swap the ring with one of the many pieces of jewelry I had from when I went through my 'trying to fit in with the vacationers' phase. I'd started thieving and thought I'd better blend in if I looked like them with brand name knockoffs and giant gems.

Being friends with the owner of Pop's Pawnshop helped since I could borrow whatever I wanted, like a ring to match Mr. Culp's.

"I don't even care about the stupid ring, I can buy another. But I want a public apology," he said. Mr. Culp shifted his gaze to me, along with the rest of the room. I chewed on my cheek and readied the explanation.

"I'm so sorry," I said. *Lie.* Only sorry that I was reckless and upset Mama. "I take off all my rings when I bake and I must have put it in my pocket next to your ring," I blurted and wrung my hands. I was good enough at lying that if I remained too calm, it'd be suspicious. "Then maybe I mixed it up with one of mine when I put it in the cake."

Mr. Culp's chiseled jaw shifted from side-to-side. The perfect shape of his face showed that his cheekbones and jawline were as fake as the ring in his fiancée's fist.

"Then, why haven't you already returned it?" he said. "Get it!"

I pulled the apron's pocket open to show him it was empty and hurried to explain that the jewelry must have slipped out. His uproar that followed sparked a white-hot rage in my chest. My mother's cautioned phrase vanished from my thoughts, and I only saw the rude couple's sins. Mr. Culp looked like an entitled rich boy who judged anyone with less money as worthless in society while his fiancée was one-hundred and ten pounds of sheer greed for instructing her company to cut benefits, then pocketing that extra change for a new nose or whatever it was she'd wasted our neighbor's lost income on.

The moment Mama stepped back and felt the real ring under her foot, I shifted to the side and positioned myself behind Mr. Culp. Delighted, Mama gasped and picked up the ring. Everybody's eyes squinted and stared at the diamond to determine if it was the right piece of jewelry. I used the split second to slip my hand into Mr. Culp's back pocket and tuck his wallet into the side of my leggings, where my hips already protruded at child-bearing angles. I'd practiced enough to ease the sleek wallet from his too-tight jeans without him so much as turning around. But he *did* absentmindedly pat his butt cheek. Thankfully, the chaos mixed with excitement and lingering rose-colored glasses of romance distracted him from noticing his empty pocket. Big events, displays of arrogance, and speeches served me well when I pickpocketed from rude vacationers.

Mama apologized profusely until I waved her away and took the full blame. Too little too late. My poor mother didn't deserve the treatment, but our neighbor definitely deserved Mr. Culp's extra cash. I'd return the wallet later, leaving it on the bedside table in his rented honeymoon suite.

Two wrongs didn't make a right, but it'd sure feel like it to Diana, once she'd paid her mortgage and kept the home she and her late husband had built with love and a lifetime of memories. Besides, nobody would ever know.

Except me.

And my band of outlaws, AKA Bella the Lookout and Johnny the Pawnshop Pops. They, and only they, could know about my long string of larcenies. And like me, they knew Folklore Falls residents needed us. Heck, the town itself needed us to keep the original crew here before the vacationers took over and buried the Falls' history.

"You *should* be sorry!" Mr. Culp spat. His angular jaw bulged at the edges as he gritted his teeth. "You're either stupid or a thief."

I wanted to slap myself over the recklessness of it all. I couldn't give up my life of crime, not yet, not until Diana got her house back, or Sara finished school, or Tuck could pay his business rent. I couldn't let emotions get in the way again—not like I would when I'd let anger from Brett the Bully push me into swiping his wallet when we were in high school to dole out the money to kids without lunches. It'd been years since I let emotions mess with a theft.

"Barry," his fiancée said.

I gritted my teeth and slipped the wallet back into his pocket when he turned to glance at her. As much as I wanted to deliver a chunk of cash to Diana, it was too suspicious considering Mr. Culp had already called me a thief.

His fiancée reached for his, arm and for a moment, I thought she might say something nice or calm his rage. Instead, she shot me a sharp glare and turned to the rest of the room to make an announcement.

"We will be leaving and staying at Jensen Resort from now on," she said.

No, no, no. My stomach twisted and flipped at the thought of the money Mama had just lost because of my reckless theft. How could I have let my emotions convince me to do something so stupid? I'd been dying to help Diana save her house, but it wasn't worth this.

I deserved the punch in my gut that the emptying dining hall left me with. The Culp family filed out, grumbling and spouting snarky comments along the way. Even when times were hard, I never stole or gave the money to myself or the B and B. I was a criminal, sure, but I had morals and a degree in business management that I refused to waste. I'd use my education and roll up my sleeves to earn every penny. Theft spoils were reserved for the neediest of Folklore Falls residents. The elderly, the grieving, and the sick.

I stood motionless in the nook with the morning sun beating on my back. Summer was coming, and it'd bring the wealthy to fill their empty vacation homes. I'd have more pockets to pick but fewer houses to pluck jewelry from. The uber-rich always left their dinner party diamonds in safes, and I'd spent the winter learning how to listen to the clicks until the combination whispered to me. But I hadn't had the time to act on it this past spring.

Grandpa Owl swished through the kitchen doors with half a stale waffle in hand. He waddled up to me and pulled one of his hand-sewn hankies from his shirt pocket. The tiny foxes that decorated the hanky's trim danced in my face as he waved it in front of me.

"Thank you," I said. "But I'm not crying."

"Never said you were." He took a bite of the waffle and chewed slowly, eyes on me the whole time.

"I feel awful," I said, as I finally took the handkerchief from him and balled it in my fist. Something about Grandpa Owl always made me admit more than I wanted. His quiet patience left me wanting to fill the silence. Not because I was uncomfortable, but because his look of curiosity always made me excited to share a new bit of information or feeling with him. How I'd kept my life as a criminal from him all these months was a mystery, even to me.

"It's not for squeezing," he said with a nod toward my hand.

The handkerchief uncurled as I relaxed my fingers. I looked down to see that my squeezes had left the thin fabric wrinkled. One crease went through a handstitched fox's face, which made it appear as though it was winking at me.

"You've got sugar all over your pants," Grandpa Owl said. "And on your eyebrows. And in your hair."

I wiped my fingerprints from the leggings and then dabbed at my eyebrow. "Thanks, Grandpa."

"You look just like your mother when you're sad," he said with a slight tilt of his head.

"I'm not sad," I said. He nodded, but it wasn't in agreement. The lie was as plain as the sugar on my face. This was why I avoided sensitive criminal-like subjects with Grandpa Owl. He could see through me as easily as I could look through the bay window in the breakfast nook. But he'd never see the smudges on me. I refused to let him or Mama. I'd done the same with my ex, but my boyfriends wanted more honesty in our relationships, whereas my family was comfortable seeing me as the innocent sweetheart that my mother had raised. They didn't dig for information because they'd never believe I could rob a house or snag Mister Rich's wallet right out of his brand-name jeans.

"Whatever you say, Little Robin," he said. I only allowed him and Mama to use that nickname. Grandpa Owl said I chirped and chattered like the American songbird when I was a child. I'd ramble on with colorfully imagined stories that branched off from Folklore Falls' original legend and had convinced other kids that my fabrications were true. The subtle red tint to my light brown hair solidified the nickname for Grandpa Owl a decade and a half ago.

"I don't think the hanky helped remove it from your hair," he said. The last bite of his waffle vanished with a gulp. He took the handkerchief back but waved it toward the dirty section of my hair.

"Sugar in my hair is the least of my concerns," I said. In a swift, practiced move, I grabbed for the hood of my green sweatshirt and pulled it over my head. The oversized sweatshirt left enough room to hide my ponytail, baking ingredients and all, and helped me blend in with the natural colors of Folklore Falls' foliage. Especially during the explosion of green in spring.

"Don't kick yourself too hard," he said with a pat on my back. "We all make mistakes. But I know what really happened." Grandpa Owl leaned his bald head toward me, bringing with it his coffee breath. He winked, and my stomach tanked. Every muscle in my body froze. My sweet old grandpa was never supposed to know about my thefts. Nobody beyond my band of outlaws was allowed that secret.

"You look like a robin who just saw a cat stalking her nest," he said. He straightened, and we stared at one another in a perfect match of height at exactly five feet three inches. He'd lost a few inches with age and gained the slight hunch that his back developed after hours upon hours spent huddling over his sewing projects.

I shook my head and swallowed hard. The remnants of the banana bread I'd eaten early that morning left a sweet taste in my mouth. It clashed with the sour situation.

"You don't have to hide it from me," he said.

Mama burst through the kitchen doors, leaving them swinging in her wake. In a flurry of flustered demands, she instructed Grandpa Owl to repair the handstitched squirrels in a pillowcase that had come unraveled. At least the traveler who'd stayed in that room admitted and apologized for allowing her children to use the pillows in a fluffy fight that caused the threads to come out.

Grandpa Owl agreed and sauntered off with one last smile in my direction. He couldn't possibly know. I was too careful.

Except when I'd messed up this morning.

"Fox in a henhouse," I cursed under my breath. Mama still heard it and raised her eyebrows with a glance over her shoulder at me. I instinctively followed her to the kitchen to help clean up the dishes from the big waffle breakfast, but she swiveled and pointed to the door on the other side of the room.

"Watch your mouth," she said, as if I'd said the other 'F' word. "The front door dinged. I need you to attend to the guests. And stop wearing that silly jewelry, it's not your style and it got us into a lot of trouble today."

"Understood," I said. "And I'm on it." I was eager to follow Grandpa Owl and pick at what he thought he knew. We parted ways, and I emerged from the dining room at the exact moment the Culps stomped down the stairs with their luggage bouncing and thumping against every step.

They stormed out the front door, leaving the tiny bell jingling, the announcement of their exit. The couple waiting at the lobby desk watched but remained unconcerned by the Culps' dramatic display of huffing anger. Or at least that's the way it appeared, based on their relaxed body language and amiable smiles.

I greeted the new, nicer couple with as much bubble as I could muster. A morning mimosa would have helped, but the sugary drink wasn't my style. Good thing beer had bubbles, too.

"What can Sherwood Bed and Breakfast do for you?" I asked, as I grabbed the pamphlet I'd put together for visitors. It included all the hidden beauty our town offered and most of the secret sites, plus a full-color page with the story of Folklore Falls' legend written by yours truly.

The woman smiled and flashed her massive ring. Dozens of diamonds encircled the thick one in the center that almost left me blinded. I'd had my fill of engagement rings, but the romantic quaintness of our B and B haunted me.

"It's our second honeymoon," her husband said, as he looked his wife up and down like he wanted to pick her up and throw her on the desk. "But it feels like our first. We'd like the biggest suite you have."

By the cut, clarity, and size of the gems on her hand, I knew this couple rivaled the Culps in wealth, though they behaved nothing like them. They wore simple, comfortable clothes, showed interest in the hiking trails I suggested, and said *both* please and thank you.

"You know so much about the legend. Do you do tours?" she asked.

"Me?" I'd never thought of it before, but telling the story while guiding people along the trails sounded delightful. I liked this woman already. Most of the elite vacationers claimed the legend of Folklore Falls wasn't history though they'd speak about the diamond dagger as if it were real. They didn't believe that hard work and true love were the source and reason for the beauty of the falls but I knew Grayson Baird carved the falls for his bride centuries ago.

The pamphlet included all the details of the long-ago love story, even the knife. I'd seen the blade and I swore to track it down and donate it to a museum where it belonged. The knife, or dagger, that I knew had been taken by one of the vacationers based on the gossip I'd heard. Snobs loved to brag, which made my quest all that much easier.

"Is this true?" the man asked, looking over the pamphlet. "What an epic story."

"They say people will do anything for true love," I said.

The chime of the front door's bell overshadowed my cliched phrase. I knew nothing about love, true or not, but the glances exchanged between this couple looked about as close as I'd get to understanding.

Between them, I caught sight of the guest who'd just entered. A man with broad shoulders turned after gently closing the door behind him. By the size of his arms, it looked like he wouldn't be able to do *anything* gently. He ran his hand through his dark waves to pull away the hair from hanging in his face. A sigh escaped him, and he glanced around to take in the homemade surroundings. He locked eyes with me, and I would have averted my obvious stare, but the determination in his gaze hooked me.

Creases of concern lined the edges of his eyes as he narrowed them. I knew that look. I'd had it many times myself. Razor-focus. He was a man on a mission, but for that split second, it seemed my stare had derailed his attention.

He mustered what might have been considered a smile, with one corner of his lips curved slightly. Or it could have been the scar that cut across the edge of his mouth like King Arthur's sword, if the scar was the blade and his chin the rock that held it. The smile vanished as fast as it came and didn't pique my curiosity so much as the fact that he looked nothing like any of our guests. His dark clothes, grumpy eyes, and purposeful gait didn't match a man on vacation.

I snapped my attention back to the guests in front of me and nodded. "I have good news," I said. "The honeymoon suite just opened back up. But we'll need about an hour to clean it properly."

"We'd love to reserve it," the woman said with a glittering smile. I strived to be like her someday, charismatic and friendly. I had my moments, but it seemed to come naturally to her. "We'll return this evening after a tour of the town."

They thanked me and passed the man with the arms. Before I could greet him, Mama intercepted, swooping in from the dining-room door. She welcomed him, and I stepped into the shadows of the staircase.

I needed to hurry and find out what Grandpa Owl knew. Not to mention, I had to make a stop at Jensen Resort and slip a few chips from gambling brunchers who had too much booze in their orange juice then make it to Diana's to drop off the steal. I didn't have the ring to save her house, but at least I could help her make this month's mortgage payment.

And on top of that, the pressure of the countdown to summer weighed heavily. I had approximately a month until the wealthy arrived at their vacation homes and until Jensen Resort's grand reopening event was held on their personal estate.

I swore the Jensens took the artifact from the Folklore Falls legend, though I needed to rule out some of the other sketchy families. While their motivation and the event itself didn't make sense to me, I'd made it my quest to get the dagger back. We'd petition to sell the diamond dagger to a museum, preserve the history I loved so much, and—best of all—donate that money to the townsfolk who needed it.

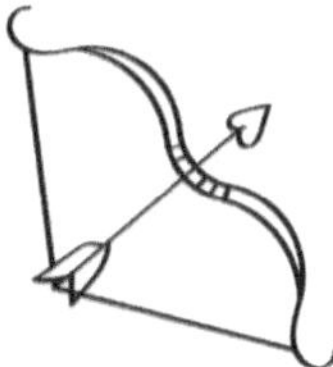

Three

The snores of Grandpa Owl asleep on the porch convinced me to change up my order of operations. I'd never liked math anyway, not unless it directly related to calculating the details of a steal.

I hopped off Sherwood Bed and Breakfast's front steps and headed down the only paved road in Folklore Falls, the one the vacationers insisted be smoothed with cement to make their drive from their original homes to their summer houses.

The walk to our neighborhood only took twenty minutes with one or two tacked on for my quick slip up to Diana's wrap-around porch. I tucked the bag of hundred-dollar bills under the edge of her doormat that read *Howdy y'all*, so that it wouldn't tumble away in case the wind picked up. Spring could be moody with the weather, and I didn't want to take the risk of losing all that cash.

I slipped away, darting into the bushes on the side of her house and then skipped back to the dirt road that lined the rural neighborhood. Thankfully, the houses in our area were spread wide enough that I didn't need to wait for the cover of nightfall to make the drop. Nobody saw me, and if they did, it'd be from a distance.

My heart should have felt considerably lighter without the stolen cash weighing me down or the worry that our neighbor would be forced to sign away her house tonight.

Instead, two things nagged at me as I kicked a rock along the road. This spring's moods brought more sunshine than usual, which meant the vacationers could arrive earlier than they had last summer.

And the mysterious man with the scar. He didn't fit with anyone else who'd ever stayed at the B and B, and it unsettled me.

People didn't come to Folklore Falls with a plan. They came to Folklore Falls to get away from their plans, and that made it easier to pick their pockets. With their guards down, I snatched Rolexes and pearl bracelets, but only according to my code. Kind people, wealthy or not, were never the target of my thefts. I'd only take from people like the Culps.

The rock tumbled off the side of the road, and I stepped on concrete. I followed the main pathway back to Sherwood, ready to confront Grandpa Owl and possibly sneak a peek at the mysterious man. His weird almost-smile and look of determination made me want to know why he'd come to our tiny town.

My stomach tightened when I rounded the hedges that lined the road and Sherwood Bed and Breakfast came into view. Folklore Falls' sheriff shook Grandpa Owl's hand in an unnecessarily testosterone-filled grip. Poor Grandpa wrung his hand out afterward, but it seemed Sheriff Max didn't notice as his mouth kept moving.

I shifted to the side to walk in the shadow of the trees on the edge of the dirt parking lot.

Did Grandpa Owl call the police when he found out I'd stolen the engagement ring? I stepped behind a tree, but he'd already noticed movement in the forest that gave our B and B its name.

"Loxley," he shouted. Sheriff Max turned around. I winced and expected pinched brows and a waggling finger of accusation. He was a good man, kind and patient, maybe even a little lazy, but we'd had our issues in the past. I never liked that he'd blamed me for spray painting his name with two extra X's on Trundle bridge out by the highway overpass. I never broke the law without a purpose, and I had zero skill with a can of aerosol paint.

Sheriff Max's expression remained unreadable. Plain. Maybe to lure me in, or maybe because he was bored and had only come by for a chat with the town seamster. Grandpa Owl had repaired the sheriff's shirt more than once when his weight gain had popped off a few buttons.

Maybe if I didn't run and came in easily, they'd agree not to tell Mama. What would I say when he locked me in jail? I forced my feet toward the porch and up the steps.

"Sheriff Max needs to speak with you," Grandpa Owl said. My heart skipped a beat, and I resisted the urge to run. "I'll leave you two alone." The comment came with a wink from Grandpa.

My stomach turned, and a whole new worry left me frowning. More than once, Grandpa had tried to set me up with some men around town. He insisted I was lonely and that I would enjoy joking with a date over sour beers. Once, he'd gone so far to suggest that I should take a man to the archery range and give my date a lesson. My grandfather was a romantic, just like his daughter. It seemed Mama had soaked all the tendency for roses and wine and public proposals in her generation and left me dry.

"No need," Sheriff Max said, and I blew out a breath. *Thank goodness.* "I just came to remind the little lady that her time is up."

My shoulders dropped. I'd forgotten about the community service I owed Folklore Falls' police department after accidentally destroying the ridiculously expensive trellis and windows on the backside of Jensen Resort. I'd told him I wrecked it out of frustration for the resort taking town jobs, and it wasn't entirely a lie.

"Perhaps you'll think twice next time you want to take your anger out on someone else's property," he said with a sniff. It didn't take a lot to convince him I'd vandalized the resort based on emotional turmoil rather than the fact that I made a mistake when trying to scale the trellis and break in for a few petty thefts. He already believed I enjoyed the destruction of property since he'd never caught the real serial spray painter.

"It was dumb," I admitted. That was the truth and nothing but the truth. *Perhaps* I had acted with emotional turmoil, just as I did today when I stole the ring without proper research and thought. "How long do I have?"

"Well." He sniffed again and pulled up his pants. They always slipped off his nonexistent butt since he couldn't fit them around his heavy waist. "I told you I'd give you options. You have a day to decide what you'd like to owe me. Trash pickup for three weeks or repaint the dividing lines on the main road. I reckon the latter will take you upwards of a month since we don't have the newfangled machine that does it automatically. We both know you're talented with paint."

I rolled my eyes and shook my head. "You'll never let it go."

"You're a good lady, Loxley," he said. "But we all make a mistake or two." His warm smile should have calmed me, but the timeline left me itching. I didn't have three weeks or upwards of a month. The vacationers would arrive soon, and I needed that time to find the legendary diamond dagger and sell it to a museum. Minor thefts helped people here and there, but the resort threatened to destroy the livelihood of hundreds of residents if it added the attractions it had planned.

"Make your decision and give me a ring," he said with his thumb and pinky sticking out and his hand shaking beside his ear. With that, he held his pants as he stepped from the porch and sauntered away.

"Speaking of a ring," Grandpa Owl started.

And the stomach-clenching returned. It didn't help that I was starving since my pathetic breakfast was hours ago.

"You don't need to blush," he said.

I didn't realize my face had heated. Maybe I was losing my stealthiness.

"Admiring the pretty ring on your finger isn't a crime. I don't blame you for being curious."

All at once, the clenching flopped, and it seemed my whole body would melt into a puddle of relief. Grandpa Owl would have to hose me off Sherwood's porch before the guests stepped on me.

"See?" he said, bringing me close with his arm around me. He guided me to the pair of rocking chairs to the left of the front door. "Doesn't it feel better to admit that you might enjoy a little pepper jack?"

"Pepper jack?" I asked, as I took a seat and let the chair rock back and forth. The creak of wood against wood instantly left me wanting a nap.

"Cheese," he said, as if that clarified anything. "All romance should have cheese with a little kick. Love and passion keep life exciting. You're not just meant to schlep around here helping your mother and I tend to guests all day before returning to your empty home."

"It's not empty—" I brought up my usual defense about the betta fish that kept my bedside table lively. Grandpa wasn't having it.

"Odette and I have experienced the joy of family and marriage."

I snorted. Joy. *Right*. Mama suffered neglect from my father for years. He was in love with his job and finally left her for it when I was in the eighth grade.

"And I hope she'll experience it again, but you, Little Robin, should branch out. Folklore Falls isn't doing you any favors. Go meet someone and bring him back here. Wouldn't it be nice to have a date at the Jensen's Grand Reopening Gala? Or if you want to meet someone from here, I know Mayor Richard is single."

I stopped rocking and turned my head to look at him.

"No, thank you." I laughed. "Politics is the last place I want to be." Though I could lie as easily as anyone in office and admired how well Mayor Richard tried to preserve the originality of our town, I didn't want to date him.

"Okay, okay," he said, throwing his hands up in surrender.

"I've told you before, and I'll tell you again. I love it here. The town is plenty of family for me." And a date for the Gala was the last thing I needed. A man would only get in my way from using the event as an opportunity to case the place for the dagger.

Grandpa Owl reached for his sewing basket and set the half-repaired pillowcase in his lap. He adjusted his glasses on his nose and set to work, threading the needle.

"Just tell me you're happy," he said, "and I'll never bring it up again."

I scooted to the edge of the chair and put my hand on his forearm. He paused the threading to look up at me over the glasses.

"I'm happy," I said. "Promise." *Not a lie*. But it also wasn't the truth. If I met the right man in the right situation, I'd get married in a heartbeat. Grandpa Owl's love for grandma had always been a joy I wanted to experience. And though they met and married within a matter of weeks, their passion remained for decades—only growing stronger with time. The reality was, my current lifestyle did not suit a relationship. So, I'd resorted to keeping romance at a distance.

He nodded and patted my hand. "Good, now see about helping your Mama get a guest settled. Gideon, I think his name is. He's found something wrong with every room she offers him."

I agreed and stood, hurrying inside. The grumpy eyes observation I'd had was spot-on. This Gideon guy had an agenda. I'd set aside just enough time to appease his complaints in consolation to what I'd done to my mother that morning, then I needed to get a lead on the diamond knife. Based on my past research, I'd narrowed down the potential takers as one of three vacationers: the Tamsens, the Evanses, or the Jensens.

Once I found Mama, she assured me Gideon had found a comfortable room but that I was welcome to check in with him at the bachelor suite that overlooked Sherwood Forest.

The suggestion came with a heavy hint drop. She thought a check-in was necessary. I climbed the staircase and made my way to the North side of the building.

The door to his room was cracked open, so I took the liberty of a peek. I scanned the basics. The couch, coffee table, bed behind that, and right there, hanging on the key hooks, was holster meant for a gun. But the gun was missing, and a shiny, curved dagger was in its place.

A slight gasp escaped me, and I looked around to be sure nobody saw or heard me.

It couldn't be *the* dagger. Could it?

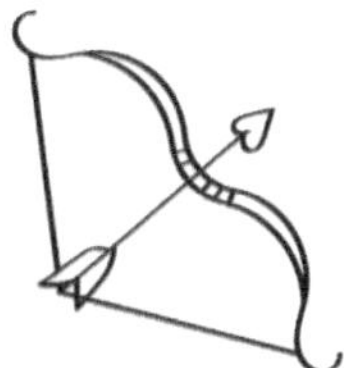

Four

Nothing was ever as easy as thrusting my hand through an open door, then darting down the hallway with the spoils tucked into the front pocket of my hoodie. And that included this theft.

After waiting for sounds, I slipped my arm into the crack between the door and the wall. I'd determined nobody was inside based on the lack of noise and movement as I peered into the room.

Now that I could focus, I saw that the little knife in the gun holster was exactly that, a weapon replacing another weapon—not the carving dagger used by Grayson Baird. This blade looked shiny, and would likely cut skin, but wasn't used by the legendary hero to carve the falls for his lover. One brush of my fingertip against the surface told me that this wasn't cut from a diamond. To be sure, I carefully lifted it out of the holster and positioned it between my teeth to feel for brittleness.

This was solid metal, not a honed, magical gem. Of course, Mama had suggested to me once that such an item didn't exist. She'd treated me like I believed in Santa Claus for acknowledging the truth in the legend.

I tipped the knife on its point and dropped it back into the holster. Disappointment left me sighing and glancing around the room. This wasn't Grayson Baird's dagger. The shiny pocket watch abandoned on top of the gym bag beside the door lifted my spirits.

I double-checked my surroundings with a quick visual pass of the hall and the room. The bathroom door was closed, which would have worried me except I noted the darkness in the crack at the bottom. Who'd sit on the toilet in the dark? The bedspread was ruffled as though someone had sat on top of it but didn't pull the covers down. Nothing else was unpacked from the gym bag other than the watch, and the holster and shoes hanging from the key hooks. Who hangs shoes?

I shook my head and crouched to examine the pocket watch. It was old, really old, which could bring its worth either upwards of a hundred thousand or squat depending on if it was rare or just a piece of junk.

Rare or not, I didn't intend to steal it. I had no reason to believe this Gideon character owed anyone anything. Not yet anyway.

"But I'll be keeping my eye on you," I muttered. Something else inside the bag caught the glint of the sunlight streaming through the window. I felt less like a Robin pecking for worms and more like a crow collecting shiny objects. I returned the pocket watch to the top of the plain gym bag, then pulled back the rest of the zipper to reveal the source of the second shine. A badge lay atop a pile of perfectly folded clothes.

A cop's badge.

Fox in a henhouse. I need to run in case he comes back.

The grinding zipper sound broke the silence as I closed the bag halfway, determined to leave everything exactly as it was. I never rushed because rushing looked suspicious, but I moved with a purpose when the situation called for it.

The pocket watch slipped over the side of the bag, so I picked it up and tried to lay it down on top with the chain arranged as it had been before. The heavy metal circle sunk into the loose fabric and flattened the top of the bag. Despite its tattered appearance, the gym bag didn't stink. In fact, it smelled like vanilla musk with a hint of saltwater.

Before I could take another whiff, the bathroom door swung open.

I leaped to my feet and took a step toward the hallway, but a dripping arm shot out and slammed the door shut before I could slip past. The room was small, sure, with the bathroom close to the front, but I didn't expect him to cover the distance in one giant step.

"See something you like?" he asked. Gideon stood with one hand splayed on the door and the other holding the towel around his waist. The heat from his post-shower body made me wish the rooms came with overhead fans.

It was definitely the scar that made him look like he had a perpetual smirk on his face. Definitely. Maybe.

I held my breath, unsure of how to respond to such a suggestive comment. What I *saw* was a mostly naked man dripping wet and steam from the hot bathroom curling around him. The arrogance in his question only intrigued me. I liked a good challenge, and bringing this jerk down a notch could be my next one.

I lifted my chin to appear bigger, though I stood several inches shorter than him.

"I prefer a man in a suit," I said. *Lie.* "And with short hair. Totally buzzed." *Massive lie.* But that would show him. Was he really so presumptuous to think I'd broken in for him?

His dark brows pinched, and he peeled his palm off the door to stand straight. He folded his arms across his chest and stood with wide feet.

"I meant the pocket watch," he said with a nod toward the gym bag.

All at once, my muscles relaxed. *Oh.* Was that all this was? *He just thinks I'm a thief, not a flirt.* I released a puff of air that sent my escaped strands of hair outward.

He thinks I'm a thief! I straightened and stifled a small gasp. The stupid thick walls had blocked the sound of his shower and I'd wrongly assumed the lack of light meant nobody was home.

"I don't know what you're talking about," I said. It was my go-to phrase when I'd lost track of the conversation. This happened often when I'd tried to keep up with the mind-numbing gossip amongst the wealthy vacationers. Eventually, I'd given up daytime pickpocketing in favor of nighttime steals so that I could avoid both blending in and the awful small-talk.

"You picked up the watch," he said, "then put it back. Is it not expensive enough for your taste?"

"Too expensive," I said. "I only wear costume jewelry." I waved my hand in his face where the pawned engagement ring had turned my finger green.

"That's not what I meant," he said. The steely gaze of his eyes fixed on mine challenged me not to blink. I stared back, as fierce as ever. He wanted me to admit I was tempted to pocket the watch. Ha. *Pocket the pocket watch.*

I chuckled at my internal joke, as terrible as one Grandpa Owl might tell.

Gideon took a step closer, and his frown deepened, though the scar still made his mouth look lopsided. My low-key laugh only seemed to piss him off.

"I have a few questions for you," he said.

"Oh?" I said, feigning disinterest, though it was a struggle not to glance down to see if the towel had stayed in its intended place. Interest was *all* I had. Though, it would be fleeting once I got into the right headspace and refocused on my timeline and the people who needed me.

"Do you often break into other peoples' hotel rooms?" he asked.

"The door was open," I said before he'd even finished the potentially accusatory question.

Gideon sniffed and narrowed his eyes. "Does an open door denote an invitation to you?"

"I don't—"

"And does a piece of someone else's property no longer count as their property if they're not actively using or wearing it?"

"Hey!" *Careful, Lox.* I'd already let emotional recklessness mess up the morning, I didn't need it wrecking my afternoon, too. I cleared my throat and lowered my voice from pitchy squeal to smooth operator. "Isn't it a little derivative to accuse the maid of the crime?"

That sent his eyebrows sky-high. He quickly adjusted his face to hide the shock from my calm quip.

Getting caught now and then was all part of the job. That was why I'd honed my tongue and skill with words. Even when I'm at my most careful, I couldn't predict everything. But I could smooth-talk my way out of what I ran into.

It seemed Gideon did the same. But I'd risen to the challenge.

"I work here," I said. *Not a lie.* "I noticed a smell coming from your room." *Still not entirely untrue.* "And I thought I could clean up the room until I noticed the source was your gym bag." *Definitely a lie now.* At least the cleaning part. "So, forgive me for trying to do my job." I mustered emotion, holding my breath for a moment and willing tears to my eyes. Sometimes it worked. I felt the wetness line the edges of my eyelids. *Bingo.*

He coughed and uncrossed his arms. The towel had slipped, revealing his hip bones. He balled the fabric into his fist to keep it tight against his skin and took a step back.

"Look," he said. "I'm on high alert regarding a continuous crime here in Folklore Falls."

Not an apology. So, he still suspected me. But the fleeting softness in his eyes told me I'd fallen far down the list.

"I caught wind that the criminal has been near this inn recently," he said. When he raked his fingers through his hair it only held back the unruly waves for a moment before they fell into his eyes again. By the thickness of his hair, I judged him to be around thirty years old, not yet of thinning age. "Since you work here, I'd appreciate a moment to sit down with you and ask about it."

I snapped my attention from his hair back to his eyes. "I've met my interrogation quota for the year," I said with a shrug. No way would I let him try to manipulate me into a confession again. For all he knew, I was as innocent as Grandpa Owl.

"No, no," he said, "not like that. I mean, I'd like to see what you know. Or if you'd recommend someone else in the hotel—"

"What's it about?" I asked. The interruption was calculated—intended to pivot his attention away from speaking with other Sherwood employees. If Gideon shared the details of the larceny with Mama, she might notice some similarities with the times I've come in late for early shifts. I couldn't risk it.

When he licked his lips, his tongue left a sheen across them. *Focus, Lox.* I gave myself a little shake. My bundled hair had slipped from the claw and tickled the back of my neck. It caused an involuntary shudder throughout my body.

Gideon's eyebrows pressed together, but he didn't acknowledge it and jumped into the explanation instead.

"I'm investigating a thief," he said.

Fox in a henhouse. I'd hoped my crimes hadn't garnered enough attention and maybe he'd arrived to catch the Jensen family committing fraud or the Culps for their snobbery. Snobbery deserved a hefty fine in my book of opinions.

"Right." I nodded. "So, you know there's a thief in the area, but you left your door open and valuables out?"

"Observant," he said with raised brows. Apparently, I'd impressed him. Not that I cared. "It's a bit of bait."

Bait? So, the pocket watch was supposed to tempt me?

"This thief is tricky. Notorious even," he said. His chest expanded and released with a sigh that brought the scent of mint. "I'm trying to think out of the box."

"Okay," I said. Why did he feel the need to explain himself to little old me? My eyes dropped to his hand, where he was twisting and wringing the corner of the towel at his waist. When he tightened it, the fabric pressed against his tawny skin. His stomach wasn't a six-pack of hard abs, but it looked muscular enough to break my knuckles if I needed to punch him. Not that I punched people, not since Brett tried to kiss me in the fifth grade. Though, I came close when Mr. Culp left a bruise on Grandpa Owl's face with the misguided toss of his Bentley's keys.

Gideon followed my gaze and glanced at the white towel around him.

"It's a good thing I don't have any pockets to pick," he said. An awkward chuckle followed the comment. The dorky joke didn't match his demeanor, and it seemed like a window was uncovered. His face even lightened for the occasion, and the sideways smirk became more than just the scar's pull on his skin. "You know? Because of the thief." He pulled at the towel.

It was my turn to raise my eyebrows. I willed the heat in my neck to subside.

"I think I should leave now," I said. I turned from him and twisted the doorknob. He backed away from the door with an uncomfortable shuffle and flustered agreement.

"Yeah, yes," he said. His gaze flickered to my hand, and he paused. "I'm sorry."

I followed his line of sight to the ring on my finger, the one almost identical to the future Mrs. Culp's.

"I'm not married," I said. *What in the—*

"Do you have a moment?" he asked. I couldn't answer. My brain still spun from the weird confession I'd just spewed. Why did I say that? Suddenly, I wanted distance between me and the half-naked man.

I crossed the threshold and turned to face him. The kind second-honeymooning couple passed me with a nod and a smile.

"For the questions about the thief, I mean," he said.

"Right now?"

Gideon hiked the towel higher. "I'll get dressed. Of course."

Hmm. I could learn what he knew and pinpoint exactly how to avoid him. This little chat could save me from getting caught. But he wasn't Sheriff Max, the cliche donut-eating small-town cop who spent more time gabbing with civilians than writing tickets. If I let anything slip, I could incriminate myself and grand larceny would stick me with a punishment far worse than painting highway lines or picking up trash.

"Okay," I agreed. But I wanted control of the situation. Our little chat didn't need to be on Sherwood grounds just in case it worried Mama or Grandpa Owl put two and two together with my mishap regarding the Culps' ring. "Meet me at Fryer Tuck's."

The slight quirk of his head told me he was definitely an outsider. Everybody knew Tuck and his famous grease fries.

My stomach groaned at the thought of them. I needed a basket of potato-y goodness and a quick nap before my long night of tracking down the dagger.

Maybe Gideon could unwittingly lead me to that, too.

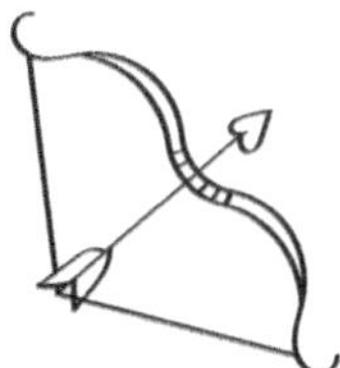

Five

Tuck plopped a milkshake in front of me, and I felt like a teenager waiting for a date. Sometimes the late-night escapades made me feel younger and dumber than I should be at twenty-six, with a degree in business, my home, and a retirement plan. But that little tickle of embarrassment was worth it to help my Folklore Falls family.

The foamy whipped cream sank into the chocolate ice cream as I swirled the straw. I glanced out the window to see Gideon approaching from the dirt road that ran behind Sherwood and down the strip of shops. Fryer Tuck's sat right in the middle of the laundromat and Bella's Bookstore that had survived Jensen Resort's patron-sucking soul. The resort didn't house a bookstore or library, yet.

Gideon's nose scrunched as he squinted from the mid-afternoon sun. The mild weather would shift by the end of the month, bringing the type of tourists I appreciated—those who stayed at a quaint inn like Sherwood, swam in the river, and showed genuine interest in the Love Dagger Legend.

I planned to ask the cop if he intended to interview any of the wealthy vacationers. If so, perhaps I'd set a date with him after his investigations. I'd never flirted my way to answers before, but I'd seen Baird's dagger once, and I knew it was real. I would not let a snobby vacationer keep it from a museum where it could be enjoyed by all. Plus, it'd teach everyone the history of our town, and in a small place like this, history, friends, and family were everything. Of course, flirting for answers would require I learn how to flirt.

The diner's door jingled with the same pitchy tune as Sherwood's bell when Gideon yanked it open. He stomped inside and stared me down. I offered a curt wave and a slight smile. His frown lines and pinched brows looked like he was somewhere between total grump and constipation, and it made me want to ditch him. Since Jensen Resort wrecked Folklore Falls, I didn't have the patience for negativity and unnecessary stress.

"It's a restaurant, not a prison," I said, as he marched up. Gideon shot me a glare as he slid into the orange vinyl bench on the other side of the booth. "I'm just saying, you don't have to look like you want to knock my milkshake off the table."

"I take my job seriously," he said.

I took a sip of chocolaty goodness and raised my eyebrow, my gaze on him the whole time. "Well, here we have french fries, not violent criminals." *Not a lie.* I was only violent with the hay-filled targets at the archery range. If we'd met three doors down at Knight's Tavern, his wariness might have been justified. Townsfolk had gotten in more than a few fights at that bar, but it was never anything more serious than a pool game mishap. Except that time when the local tattoo artist, Katrina, had 'accidentally' stabbed Bones with a dart because he didn't ask her on a date.

"I'm not a fan of potatoes," he said, as he slapped the menu down and raised his hand. Tuck sauntered over. By the time the cook reached us, he huffed and puffed. Grease stains covered his undersized shirt. Tuck only employed a server on the weekends when it got busy after Folklore Fall's High School football games. During the rest of the week, he stood behind the fryer and the locals would shout orders to him from their tables. Unfortunately for all of us involved, Gideon wasn't a local, and it required Tuck to emerge from his cave of grease and potatoes.

Speaking of, who doesn't like potatoes? And hangs up their shoes?

Psycho. But a useful psycho. I needed to find out what he knew, then I could ditch him and leave the grumpy fry-hater behind.

Once he'd ordered the chicken wrap, Gideon turned to me and leaned his elbows on the table. The old tabletop tilted under his weight, and I had to grab my glass to stop the milkshake from sliding away.

"I intend to bring this thief in before the end of the week," he said.

Good luck.

"Into Sheriff Max's cell?" I asked. Our local police department housed only one cell, and it was reserved for the town drunk, Grandpa Owl's friend Falstaff. Poor Gramps had tried to convince Falstaff to replace his alcoholism with sewing, and it'd earned him a week of the silent treatment.

"Ha." Gideon scoffed. "No, this criminal will be put on trial in the city and taken to a maximum-security prison."

I forced myself to swallow an icy chunk of the milkshake. It scratched my throat on the way down and I tried not to grimace.

"For taking a few TVs?" I purposely added an item I'd never stolen. Who wants to yank a flatscreen off the walls these days? Gems and EarPods were worth plenty and were easy to slip.

"Grand larceny is grand larceny," he said without consideration to gray areas. "It serves them right."

Ugh. You don't even know why I'm stealing.

It was a good thing Tuck returned with Gideon's order. The fryer plopped the plate on the 1950s style tabletop and sauntered off without a word. It took everything I had not to launch my milkshake at the cop and slip out while he wiped whipped cream out of his eyes.

I needed to stay calm and pick his brain or shift his focus to the *real* missing treasure. So, I nodded through the boring stuff while I polished off my drink. He took police work seriously, but not as seriously as I took helping the needy. The rules and laws and policies were a jumble of legal jargon that told me he had zero charisma and even less personality. When a person bases their entire identity on something external, like their wealth or job, that was when I tuned out.

"The suspect has been targeting this area for several months now and has evaded local police," he said.

And always will. Sheriff Max might suffer an angry word or two from disgruntled vacationers, but he never seemed to care. Plus, the targets of my theft had upped their security game with extra cameras and alarms. So, where did Gideon come from?

"I've never seen you around here before," I said.

Gideon bit into the chicken wrap, the most boring item on the menu. I didn't have patience for boring. Maybe that was what I loved about the legend of Folklore Falls so much—not the romance, but the adventure behind it. Grayson Baird fought bears and unknown creatures to carve the falls and prove his worthiness.

"I'm from up East," he said. "I've been, uh." He paused and stared at the perfect half-circle of a bite he'd taken out of the wrap. "I've been relocated."

"You're lucky."

Gideon snorted and shook his head.

"I'm serious," I said. I wanted to swipe the snark off his face. "Folklore Falls is the best place to live."

"I'm not staying," he said with a mere glance at me. *Ugh.* I should have known he was just like my ex. I attracted a *type*, unfortunately, that included dark hair, obnoxious frowns that I saw as a challenge to turn upside down, and emotionless men. Apparently, I'm a sadist. Or I'd just stay single, forever. That was the smartest choice. "I just got assigned to this case because my work was slipping. Sorry—" he glanced at me and scrubbed his palm over his face before releasing a sigh. "I don't know why I'm telling you this."

"I have that way with people. It's why I usually work the front desk at Sherwood." I took another sip of the milkshake. It was true except when it came to people like the Culps. I cringed at the memory of this morning.

"Have you observed anything unusual?" he asked. "The thief seems to steal from those who come from out of town."

"I know there's a missing dagger," I said, to see his reaction. Gideon only nodded.

"I'll add it to the list," he said. "Do you know who they stole that from?"

"The town," I said. Tuck returned with my order, a heaping plate of steaming fries. The grease smelled simultaneously delicious and like a stomachache waiting to happen. I picked several up anyway, then thought better of it and put them back down. If I needed to flirt my way around Gideon later, I might need to be on my best behavior now.

"The town?" he asked.

"Yes," I said, as I dipped the fry in ketchup. "We don't have a museum. Not yet. But we're going to someday and the dagger belongs there."

"Is it valuable?"

"It's made of diamond," I said.

"A dagger made of diamond? Sounds useless."

"You sound useless!" I snapped, then quickly chomped into another fry and turned my face away. What the heck was wrong with me? I'm a smooth-talker. I've slipped out of so many situations with a sharp tongue and yet this grumpy out-of-towner pissed me off enough to lose my cool. Heat rose to my cheeks over the appearance of my temper.

He *was* becoming more and more useless to me now that I discovered he didn't know a thing about the dagger. But I needed to calm down since he could still give me information about the vacationers. Plus, I didn't hate talking to him, and I couldn't put my finger on why.

"I'm kidding," I said. "But that dagger is important to our history, and it's missing. If you're not investigating that, why even come here?"

"I'm here to bring a criminal to justice."

Justice. I laughed, and he frowned deeper, if that was even possible.

"Right," I said. "And what about the Jensen's Resort that came in and destroyed our entire town? Where's the justice for all the locals who lost their businesses? Jensen Estate grounds has already bought up too much land from the locals, then they came rampaging in with a massive resort. I played in that forest before their estate chopped it down. I knew the area like the back of my hand before they came in a changed everything."

Gideon straightened. He put the rest of the wrap down on the plate and pushed his lunch away. His steady gaze came with a slight crease between his brow.

"What?" I asked.

"I'm just listening," he said.

"Is this some kind of interrogation tactic? I told you I'm just an employee at Sherwood."

He leaned forward and crossed his arms on the table. His gray eyes looked like a storm in both intensity and color.

"Nobody is just any one thing," he said. It wasn't poetic, but it caused me to pause. I could argue it with a complete list of snobs who are nothing but their brand names and overpriced convertibles. "You seem to be really passionate about this town."

"And you make it sound like the only thing that matters is the junk people lost to the thief," I said.

"That is my investigation," he agreed.

"What about the real valuables?"

"Like what?" he asked.

"Folk's homes and family businesses."

"I don't know how to help with that," he said. *Typical.* He probably didn't care, either.

I jabbed another fry into the ketchup, but it came up with only a tiny red dot on the tip. The condiment cup ran dry, and I was ready to hurry this conversation along.

"Except I'd like to," he said.

I almost dropped the fry.

"But I can't help anyone do anything unless I finish my investigation and keep my job," he said. He leaned to one side and pulled a small pad of paper from his back pocket, then flipped to a blank page and produced a pen from who-knows-where. "Now, have any of the guests experienced a theft while staying at the inn?" he asked.

"No." *Lie.* But the Culps didn't count since they got their ring back, right? "I'm sure you already know where the thief targets?" I asked, fishing for information.

"Yes, the type of people with expensive junk." He used my word, and I realized he was actually listening, not just letting me rant as

Johnny and Bella did, or my ex. And it wasn't just for his investigation. "What's really valuable here is that people feel safe in Folklore Falls, junk-owners or not."

I chewed on my cheek and watched as he took notes from the rest of our conversation. Gideon even cracked a smile when I teased him for hanging his shoes up.

"Who does that?" I laughed.

He shrugged. "Teenagers who want their Nikes displayed on power lines?"

"And grumpy old cops."

His nose crinkled. "I'm not old."

"You carry a pocket watch!" I laughed. "And I like how you didn't deny the grumpy part."

"The pocket watch was a gift from when I became a detective," he said, before scooting to the edge of the booth and calling for Tuck. We stayed long enough that he ordered his own plate of fries, favoring the grease over his plain wrap. "It's old and has a story behind it."

"I didn't pin you as a guy who likes old things, considering they're usually not pristine. You didn't even leave your shoes on the floor."

Gideon shook his head to knock the hair away from his face and looked at me with his clear, dark eyes. "I like clean things. But I also enjoy old things because they speak of history and history is a lot like an investigation. Old items tell a story the same way evidence does. Except history doesn't always involve crime so it's a guilt-free pleasure."

took a drink of water to wash the taste of ketchup and potato away. "Ah, now it makes sense why you wanted to talk to me." I nodded. "I take after my grandfather in storytelling charisma. So, is there a story behind your old chicken wrap?" I tilted my head toward the forgotten plate.

"The safe choice was the heart-healthy meal," he said, pointing a fry at the abandoned spinach tortilla and chicken. "But I'm tired of safe."

"You say that word a lot," I said.

"Observant again," he said. "I don't always trust that people will make choices that won't endanger others. So, I do what I can to make the community safe."

I'd finished my plate, folded my arms, and sunk back into the vinyl cushion. The late afternoon demanded its nap from me with heavy eyes. I hadn't realized how much time passed, and yet, I didn't get up.

"If you ever need backup, I'm good with a bow and arrow," I said. *Why did I offer that?* I couldn't spend time with a normal guy without racking up the lies, much less a cop. But Gideon's lips curved. The sword scar vanished in the wrinkle of the warm expression. In an instant, he'd gone from cold and calculating to a small smile that I found myself wanting to make bigger.

I straightened and scooted to the edge of the bench.

"You know a lot about Folklore Falls," he said. "I appreciate you taking the time to help me out."

Help him out? Is that what I did? I took too much time doing it. I pulled my phone from my back pocket and tapped the screen. No way, it was dinnertime. The clock must have been wrong. But the buzz in Fryer Tuck's said otherwise. Somehow, I'd tuned the other diners and their conversations out.

I'd wasted my whole nap time and would need to prepare for sneaking into the three houses I planned to target that night. But I still didn't get up.

"Don't worry," he said. "I've got the check."

I nodded and thanked him with a half-smile. Finally, my legs moved. I stood and shuffled for the door.

Something about going home to my empty house felt so… boring.

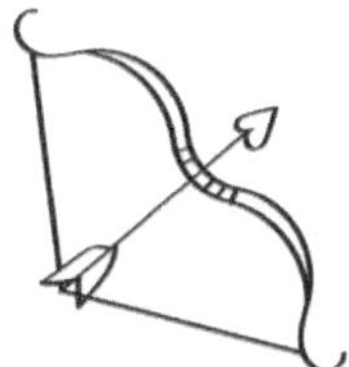

Six

The glass on the display case steamed with my breath. Random items from a puzzle box to a ruby-encrusted ladybug broach lined the shelves. Johnny pushed the curtain out of the way and emerged from the back room of Pop's Pawnshop.

"Relationships are not an adventure," I said with a yawn. After skipping yesterday's nap and staying out all night to break into the Tamsens' mansion, exhaustion had caught up with me. My inspection cleared the Tamsen family name from my list of dagger-stealing suspects.

Johnny surrendered with his palms up. "All I'm saying is that a relationship isn't boring, either."

Bella came from the back with a wad of cash and leaned on the display case. Black lipstick made her look even paler than usual but matched with her dark lace layers. She slid me several hundred dollars for the weird naked statue I'd taken from the mantle of the Hills' lakefront mansion. I'd hit their house after Mrs. Hill crashed into Katrina's parked car and drove off. She might have gotten away with the hit and run if we didn't see the Audi speed off with the license plate that read HLLSWIN.

Bella sat on the counter beside the display case and swung her legs back and forth.

"Why are we talking about relationships?" she asked. "Did someone say Johnny and I should date again?"

Townsfolk had been asking since she spent a lot of time at the pawnshop lately. Though Pop's was a good twenty minutes down the main highway in the purgatory place between city lines, Folklore Falls people still knew Johnny well enough.

"No," Johnny said. He'd conjured a dirty rag from somewhere and started wiping the smudges I'd left on the display case. It worked. I knew a little magic existed. "I said that Lox is obviously lonely as hell since she came all the way out here with only one thing to pawn."

"It's only twenty minutes," I said.

"And you never used to drive out here unless you had a whole backpack full of crap."

"Maybe I have plans to go to the Jensen Resort after this," I said. I'd hit the lobby to see if the early warm weather had drawn people into town.

"The same Jensen Resort that's in the opposite direction?" he asked.

I rolled my eyes. "My point is that I was already out driving."

"If anyone accuses me of dating this nut-bag, you'll hit them with an arrow, right?" Bella asked with her thumb pointing at Johnny. She helped at the pawnshop to earn extra cash when the bookstore was slow. The sudden increase in their time spent together sent gossip around town. And as much as I wasn't a fan of gossip, I preferred those rumors over the petty conversations among the specialized group of vacationers.

I only shook my head, and Bella sighed. Thin shoulders slumped, she hung her head, pretending to be suddenly interested in her book. The cover looked ragged, and I'd bet I wouldn't understand a word of the old English inside. But Bella devoured anything with a story.

"I'm the nut-bag?" Johnny scoffed. "You're the one who reads the same books seventeen times in a row." He wiped his hand over his bald head. The collage of tattoos looked like hair when I squinted. Someday, I'd gather the courage to get more ink of my own.

"You sleep with your socks on!" she squealed. Bella slapped her book shut and threw her arm back, threatening to toss it at him.

I pulled the sleeve of the blazer over my wrist where I'd gotten a small bow and arrow tattoo. No sense in reminding Bella about weapons in her moment of heated argumentation. But Bella was all bark. She'd learned more than a few choice words from her beloved novels and left the stabbing up to Katrina.

My friends' only crime was their loyalty to me. I worked in the shadows, carefully, to not implicate them.

"So, wait," I said, tuning back into the argument. "You go everywhere barefoot, even the hike to the falls, and yet you wear socks to bed?"

Johnny lifted his leg and plopped his foot on the table beside the display case. He wiggled his toes at us. Bella shrieked like a schoolgirl and swatted the bottom of his foot with the back of her book.

"You know what else socks are good for?" he said with a wry look on his face.

"Better sex," I answered. "You repeat yourself more often than my grandfather."

Johnny shrugged, but it looked uncomfortable in his bent position. "You'd know if you *ever* let yourself go on a date after—"

"Shh!" Bella leaned across the table and pressed her finger over his lips. "He should not be named."

"Right," Johnny mumbled.

One might see chemistry between Bella and Johnny, but one would be wrong. They fought like brother and sister if you knew them well enough—and long enough. We'd been the three musketeers since grade school when I'd con more chocolate milk from the lunch lady. Bella would keep a lookout while Johnny sold the extras to other kids, so we could pull together cash for my grandma's funeral.

"We don't talk about exes," she said.

"You're full of botched movie quotes, aren't you?" I laughed, but the *Encanto* song was already stuck in my head.

"At least I don't look like an outdated Hallmark movie version of a businesswoman," she said. Bella eyed my awful pantsuit. I'd nicked it from the lost and found when Jensen Resort first opened. It might have been a hideous blood red, but it fit my short legs and the tag that read Giorgio Armani made me virtually invisible among the vacationers.

It took some effort for the inflexible Johnny to pull his leg off the table and balance on two feet again.

"Serves you right," Bella said with her nose in the air, as he stumbled back and bumped into the wall.

The phrase left me with weird goosebumps down my neck. It was so judgmental and icky and reminded me exactly why my next "date" with the cop would only be a play for more information.

My phone buzzed. Only three people called me, and two of them were right in front of me. I hurried to pull my phone from the blazer's pocket and respond to whatever emergency my family had.

"Mama?" I answered.

"Um," a deep voice said, "this is Officer Notting,"

"Officer Notting?" I repeated.

Bella's jaw dropped.

"Officer Naughty?" Johnny mouthed. They exchanged expressions of exaggerated shock, then looked back at me with wide eyes.

"Gideon," the man on the other line said with a cough. "I apologize. I never formally introduced myself."

"How did you get my number?" I asked.

Johnny mimed typing on an invisible phone, then whispered his fake conversation. "Yes, hello, is this the strip club? I know I call you every day, but how do you have my number?"

I pinched the phone between my ear and shoulder and yanked the hair tie from my ponytail. Johnny ducked before I'd pulled the elastic back and released. But I had practiced aim with projectiles and clocked him just above his ear.

"Apparently, your local PD doesn't even lock the station when they leave," he said.

Sheriff Max must have popped out for his usual evening siesta in his car behind the station.

"That didn't answer my question," I said.

"There's a phone book," he said. "I didn't even know these still existed in print. You're the only name I recognized. Plus, uh." He paused.

Johnny greeted an incoming customer while Bella disappeared into the back with her book. In a breath, I found myself alone with Gideon. Or his voice.

"It sounds like you know the Estate well. I'd like you to show me there," he said.

I gave the phone a weird look, even though he couldn't see me. Jensen Estate wasn't easy to get to, or even find, since they'd kept just enough trees to make their property private. But it also wasn't impossible. Did he know about me? Was this a setup? And who was he to snag my number and basically demand I dedicate my precious free time to helping in his stupid investigation? But if I didn't agree, it could make me look suspicious.

"Fine," I said. I'd take him because I could use the trip to case the Estate for tonight's break-in while simultaneously staying one step ahead of Gideon.

"Good, I'll pick you up from the Inn in ten minutes."

Excuse me? "I'm not there."

"I thought it was your job," he said.

"And that means I should be there all day, every day?" *People are more than their careers.*

"I am," he mumbled. "Where can I meet you in thirty?"

He still assumed I had nothing better to do than to be his personal tour guide. And maybe if he'd asked to see the falls, I wouldn't mind.

"You can pick me up at the archery range in France," I said. I could almost hear his confusion and hurried to explain before we got into another round of lost-cop-expects-me-to-solve-his-problem. "That's what we call French Village, a road off the main highway."

Gideon sighed, and it was the auditory version of the perpetually pinched look on his face. "You don't name your highway, and the roads that do have names, are called by different names."

"Yep," I said, proud of my town. Our local quirks made Folklore

Falls unique. They made it a home. "France is the closest named street to Jensen Estate. See you in half."

I tapped End Call before he could sigh again and set me on edge. If he suspected me, he was doing a terrible job of convincing me to step into the trap. Even a criminal like me didn't like to be around that kind of negativity.

"Are you leaving?" Bella asked from behind the counter. The other outlaw in our trio had vanished into the backroom after striking a deal with the customer from earlier.

I nodded as I headed for the door. "I might not need you on lookout tonight if I can case Jensen Estate today."

"Oh?" Her mouth formed a circle, and her eyebrows popped up in thick, angular lines like the Arc de Triomphe.

"It's a long story, but I'm taking Gideon there now," I said. I twisted the door handle. Bella's eyebrows almost disappeared into her hairline now. I shrugged and stepped over the threshold and into the dim evening glow. The sky over Folklore Falls always turned orange and red when the sun set at this time of year. It was another reminder that my time was running out. I needed to find who'd taken the dagger before summer arrived. The vacationers couldn't be trusted with the piece of history. They'd probably sell it for a third house in the Bahamas or a personal jet.

"Have fun on your date with Officer Naughty!" Johnny shouted from behind the curtain that separated the small shop into two 'rooms.'

"It's not a date," I called back, but the heavy door had already swung shut behind me.

I repeated the line on the quiet drive back into town. I said it again when I arrived at the archery range before Gideon. The few extra minutes left me with time to blow off steam.

My keys clinked against one another as I yanked them from my pocket and unlocked the small shop that housed the rental archery equipment. Bones ran the range when tourists visited and wanted a novelty activity to fill their time. In the off season, I enjoyed a silent, still range where I could loose a few arrows.

The zing of an arrow, that slight rush of wind, the tension of holding my breath. Each part was my therapy.

Although the days were counting down, and the dagger was still missing, I kept my cool. I needed to throw Gideon off my scent so I could freely search for the artifact and snag a few more items from vacation homes before I'd have to resort to pickpocketing and blending into the snob crowd.

An evening breeze sent the leaves in an ocean's wave of rustling. The crashing call of the forest slowed my heartbeat. When I reached over my shoulder for another arrow, the stupid Armani suit stopped my arm short. I pushed my arm back farther and the crack of tearing fabric signaled I'd ruined another nice outfit.

"Fox in a henhouse!" I shouted. Only the trees answered with another shake of leaves. I sighed at the ripped sleeve over my right elbow and swore to ask Grandpa Owl for help later. Hopefully, he didn't know this brand by name or else he'd definitely question where I'd gotten the suit.

I nocked another arrow, blew out a slow breath, and released with my gaze fixed on the hay-filled target sixty yards away.

The arrow dug into the target, pinching the burlap fabric just outside the center circle.

"Now try that with a gun."

I spun around at the sound of the voice behind me. The deafening rush of air through the trees had concealed the sound of the cop's Civic. He slammed the car's door shut and marched toward me, his gait wide and cocky.

Says the guy with a knife in his gun holster. "No, thanks," I said with a forced smile.

"You're good at shooting," he said. Whether it was meant to be a compliment or not, I couldn't tell.

"I prefer the term loosing." I lifted the bow. "I think it suits archery better."

After locking the equipment back in the shed, I hopped into his car. Maybe I was too trusting, but his potentially murderous intentions didn't occur to me until we were out on the unnamed dirt road. I'd heard from the inner circle of vacationers that the Jensens refused to pave their road, not because it would cut through the forest, but because it added 'authenticity' in case they ever planned to sell.

I glanced at Gideon, who drove like an old lady—back pin-straight, eyes squinted, hands on ten and two. It didn't make me feel any safer, but the fact that I had my own pocketknife did. He'd definitely overpower me in size and strength, but I was wiry, knew the layout of the land, and had plenty of practice with pointy weapons. Though throwing a knife was nothing like loosing an arrow, I'd manage.

"Speaking of guns," I said, though nobody was speaking and neither of us had a gun. The silence was too creepy, like the invisible pollution of negativity. So, I broke it. "What's with the knife in the holster?" I nodded toward his waist.

"It's nobody's business but my own," he said.

"Right," I said. "And I'm only taking time out of my day to help you with your little investigation. But you can't muster enough energy to have a chat with me."

Gideon sighed and took a cautionary glance at me. His gaze returned to the road again.

"I told you, I'm focused," he said. I rolled my eyes. *Focused on the wrong thing. I'm right in front of you. Hello?* But Gideon didn't sense my thoughts or notice my own pinched expression. Not that I wanted him to. I couldn't imagine anyone desiring Oscar the Grouch's attention. Instead, his eyes widened as the estate came into view.

The mansion stood taller than the old trees surrounding the grounds that the Jensens had so kindly allowed to live. The trees that grew within the gates weren't so lucky.

When we pulled up to the gate, Gideon flashed his badge to the camera, and the housekeeper punched in the code. The gate rolled open, slowly and ominously on its track, and he inched the car forward.

Riding with a cop had its advantages. Never had I so easily entered a vacationer's overly fancy property. It normally took careful preparation, Bella's lookout expertise, and a lot of sneaking. I could get used to this. If only the cop wasn't hunting me, I might use his perks a few more times.

My heart skipped a beat at the exact moment Gideon finally spoke.

"It's hideous," he said.

I burst into an unexpected laugh.

"Yeah, and they killed a huge chunk of Sherwood Forest to build it," I said. "See what I mean by them destroying our town?"

Gideon lifted his chin, and I thought he might nod in agreement with me. Instead, he threw his door open and climbed out of the car.

"I see a target for the thief."

Seven

Gideon himself was a target for the thief. If I were the punching sort, I'd have socked him right in the Adam's apple for being so blind. He was hunting petty—okay, grand—thefts while the vacationers were murdering living things for their spas and useless gazebos.

I had to admit, the inside of the mansion almost took my breath away. Almost. The arched ceiling hung over us like that of a chapel with stained-glass skylights and two large pillars in the entryway. It was excessive, didn't match the hideous style of the outside of the building, and reminded me how selfish the family was for wiping so many small businesses out of town with their equally excessive resort.

The cop cornered the Jensen's year-round housekeeper who lived in the tiny shack on the edge of the grounds. She was the reason I'd left this estate for last. It was my trickiest break-in since they never left the house unattended.

They dove into conversation. It was like watching two old ladies squabble over book club gossip, except I found my gaze lingering on the one with the facial hair. I flicked my eyes back to the ceiling when Gideon glanced in my direction. The sun had gone now, but the colors of the stained glass picked up the glow of the moonlight.

"And you're sure nothing has been taken since last summer?"

Gideon asked. The housekeeper brought her finger to her lips and considered his question.

When I was younger and dumber, AKA at the end of last summer, I got a little buzzed on a few beers and took my anger out on the Jensens after Diana's bakery had to shutter the doors for good. I'd taken a baseball bat to the Jensen's security cameras, then whacked the head off the fountain's cherub. The head itself was pawned for a few hundred in cash, since it was made out of Jade.

The warm oranges and yellows in the glass almost tricked me into thinking this mansion was like a home. But it wasn't like the homes of the townspeople, with memories and homemade decorations, full of families and hugs and meals shared with friends. The Jensen Estate, like all the vacationers' homes, was cold, sterile, and… *empty.*

I frowned. The shapes in the glass looked abstract, or maybe like larger flowers at first, but the longer I stared, the clearer it became.

The warmer colors depicted the sunset and the cool darkness that came through from the night sky colored the mountains. A tint of blue showed the falls.

A small gasp escaped me. Absentmindedly, I stepped back, my mouth agape. I backed up to the large double doors and twisted my neck to see the full picture in the stained art.

Each window showed a different picture, starting with a woman on a throne and ending with the waterfall. In the middle, I recognized the shape of a man holding a blade.

"Grayson," I whispered.

"Gideon," Gideon shouted in my ear.

I flinched and shot him a nasty look. "Son of a biscuit. Why did you just yell at me?"

He folded his arms and pursed his lips before responding. "You said Grayson, but my name is Gideon."

"No," I said, as I pointed above us. "Look, it's the legend."

Gideon showed mild interest until the housekeeper returned with the insurance papers and photographs to show him my first steal, the cherub's head. Of course, neither of them knew the thief stood right behind them.

"Ah, yes," the housekeeper said, "the Jensens love that legend. I'd say they stake their whole claim to fame on it, though I have no idea why."

I furrowed my brows and tried to wrap my head around what that meant. Didn't their money come from a family inheritance? Their 'fame' revolved around the resort they'd built, which effectively erased the history and charm of the town. So, why the stained-glass nod to Grayson Baird and Ellery?

"Does the house have a safe?" Gideon asked.

The housekeeper nodded. "Two," she said.

"Do you have access to them?" he said.

She nodded again, and I registered the information. Two separate safes would make my job more difficult. I guessed they'd be in different locations, likely opposite ends of the house, in order to avoid valuables taken all in one robbery.

"Has anything ever gone missing from the safes?" The questions continued, and the housekeeper answered with simple one-word responses.

"May I look at the artwork?" I asked. Since she was so busy with Gideon's bombarding interrogation, she only afforded me what I might consider a slight nod. I took it and ran, or slipped rather, down the hall. Their voices echoed in the open walkways and bounced off the marble flooring.

The entryway branched into two directions with long corridors. Giant paintings lined the walls. The Jensen family eyed me through their portraits. It seemed they judged me for my inconspicuous hunt for the safes. Black oil pupils followed every step I took.

I hissed at the paintings and muttered a few choice curses at the Jensen family. The parents and two adult sons only looked down at me with carefully curated faces.

A chill ran through the corridor and sent goosebumps up my arm. I wished it was spooky rather than just sad, devoid of heart and home. At least my house had Betty the Betta.

"Where's the dagger?" I whispered up at the father. Each portrait captured their similarities. Lifeless looking or not, they were a family, and they came here every year, as a family. One of the adult sons had a wife and kids of his own. And much like the Culps, Milan and Thomas Jensen always looked at one another with love and respect. My stomach twisted with an unfamiliar feeling.

I couldn't possibly be jealous of the Jensens. Maybe I needed to try dating again—a real date, not a gathering of intel. Yesterday's lunch replayed in my mind, and the cop's words came back to me.

I'd like to understand. Was it all part of his investigation? Or did he really listen and care to know about my love for Folklore Falls?

"Who else knows the location of each camera?" Gideon's voice echoed.

"The Jensens and the security company that installed them," the housekeeper's voice turned squeaky.

"And you," he said.

I paused my walk to listen.

"Is there a cleaner or landscaper who might have tipped off the thief? Or is it only you here during the off-season?" he asked. Before she could answer, he added another suggestion. "How much did the statue's head sell for?"

What the hell was he doing? If she answered, she'd implicate herself. It was basic knowledge around Folklore Falls. Of course she knew how much someone had paid for it because it was the topic of gossip both online and in the tavern for weeks.

"How much?" he repeated.

"Uh," she said.

Gideon more or less accused the innocent housekeeper, and I felt myself fuming. Bile rose in my throat, and I had to swallow the bitter taste back down.

"Look," he said. "I'm trying to help the Jensens and the rest of the victims around town."

The vacationers as victims? Funny. Gross. *Wrong.*

"Ew." I shook off the disappointment like a dog after rolling in the mud. I had actually wanted to make Gideon smile yesterday. The thought of it now gave me a stomachache and creeped me out more than the oil paintings that stared down at me.

"I don't know," the housekeeper said. I heard Gideon sigh. The interrogation was coming to a close, and I hadn't used my opportunity. "All I can tell you is that they're due back in town the Friday before the Gala. They've an important meeting here that night, and they've paid me to be off the premises."

I hurried to open the two doors at the end of the hall. One housed a large guest bedroom, and the other had stairs to a wine cellar. I flashed the light from my phone down the steps and spotted the glint of the glow on the metal. Bingo. I'd spotted one safe.

After closing the door quietly, I stopped by the closest window and flipped the lock upward, then lifted it slightly to be sure it wouldn't trigger an alarm. I slipped back down the hall and emerged just when Gideon snapped his notepad shut. He gave me a curt wave, like I was the evil sidekick that he expected to follow in his wake.

"Let's go," he barked.

I smiled at the housekeeper and exited behind Gideon. He might think I was helping him still, but I planned an interrogation of my own for the ride back.

The car's engine roared to life, and Gideon stepped on the gas. The tires left marks on the tiny, smooth stones that lined the driveway.

"So, did you find your thief?" I asked, as we pulled through the gate.

Gideon only grunted.

Or are you mad you're further from the truth than ever? I resisted the satisfied smile that twitched on my lips.

"I have a lot more people to question," he said. With a quick glance my way, he tried to smile, but it came out like a predator baring its teeth. "Thanks for showing me here. Since you know the town so well, I'd appreciate any other suggestions."

Over my dead body. I refused to help him cater to the elite group of vacationers just so he could get his rocks off by tossing the easy target in prison. I was a criminal, sure, but I didn't kill thousands of trees, wipe dozens of businesses off the map, and virtually raise a manicured middle finger to the residents and history of Folklore Falls.

"Didn't you already accuse the housekeeper?" I said. "Sounds familiar." The last part I added under my breath, but he looked at me as though he'd heard it.

The car jostled over potholes once we reached the main road. Gideon drove in the middle like arrogant jerks do with their oversized trucks or expensive convertibles. He was no different from Mr. Culp or the Jensens. Wait, no. He was worse.

Maybe I could muster puke from my unsettled stomach and stain his stupid Civic's interior. Then, I'd blame it on his horrible driving. Trees zipped by as he sped toward the town.

"I told you I take my job seriously," he said, as if that explained his aggressive behavior toward the poor housekeeper.

Anger burned in my chest, and I knew it wasn't acid reflux this time. I gnawed too hard on my bottom lip until I tasted blood. It reminded me of when I was a kid and I'd hide quarters under my tongue after nicking the change from mean customers at the B and B.

"So that gives you the right to accuse innocent people?" I snapped. The words spilled out before I could stop them.

"How do you know she's innocent?" he said. "The facts point to her involvement so far."

"What facts? You're throwing darts at the obvious answers and hoping they stick. I can tell you right now, you are way off target."

Fox in a henhouse.

Gideon pulled the car over into a dirt alcove alongside Falstaff's apple orchard. The trees bore small unripe apples the same color as the leaves. It amazed me that the town drunk climbed those branches every spring and successfully pruned them.

"What are you doing?" I asked, as I grabbed the door handle. The locks clicked, and I worried he wanted to murder me again.

The scar twisted with his frown. It looked broken and bent.

"You know something," he said. His dark eyes searched mine, and he spoke in a calm voice that should have spooked me. It was heavy, weighted with accusation. Or was it curiosity? Like the oil painting's pupils, his eyes glittered in the moonlight that shone in the passenger window. He leaned closer, and for a second, thoughts of murder flipped like a switch, and it seemed he might dip forward to kiss me.

I resisted gagging.

"I know that you're creeping me out," I said. *Not a lie.*

"Look, I'm on a countdown," he said. The tension in his shoulders relaxed slightly. "I need to find this thief and bring him in before I'm stuck doing desk duty in this town forever."

"And like you said before," I started, "I'm too busy with my own job." *Still not untrue.*

"Understood," he said. The car shifted back into drive under the weight of his palm, and the tires spun out on the dirt. "I forget not everybody wants justice as much as I do."

"Have you ever considered you're looking in the wrong place?" I asked.

We resumed on the paved road where the dividing line was dim. The hard line of Gideon's mouth looked like he'd never once considered himself wrong in his entire life.

"I don't know what that means," he said. "And I'm not wrong. Criminals deserve to be brought to justice or else this world would never be safe."

"Safe?" I scoffed. "You think ultra-wealthy people are suffering when a tiny item in their collections goes missing? If you want to keep people safe, maybe you should look into the people you're trying to 'protect.'" I used my fingers for air quotes to drive the point home before crossing my arms.

"I'm looking for people who break the law," he said, his voice raised. The car crunched over gravel as he yanked the steering wheel, and we rumbled into the rough parking lot at the archery range.

"Well," I said, as I kicked the door open, "good luck with that." I slammed it shut and stormed across the lot toward the shed.

I'm such an idiot. Why did I open my big mouth? I was too passionate about my beliefs, and the stupid cop drove it out of me.

Speaking of driving, the cop wasn't. He sat with the Civic idling in the lot. Exhaust puffed from the back pipe and disappeared up into the night sky. I emerged from the shed just as he finally turned the car around. Though nobody was around for miles, he still flicked the blinker on to show which direction he'd turn—a rule–follower, personality-less, boring-ass, arrogant cop to his core.

I whipped an arrow from the pack on my back, nocked it, and loosed it just as the car sped forward. The arrow landed with a faint thunk into the earth just outside the Civic's tire. I'd missed on purpose.

My words implicated me enough without adding destruction of property to the list. But it didn't matter because I'd be sure never to see the jerk again. I couldn't even stomach the thought of another fake date for informational purposes.

How did I stand being around him for more than ten seconds before? Even if he wasn't an arrogant prick, he'd never like me—especially not if he knew who I really was.

The sound of the car's engine faded, and I sighed, puffing breath into the darkness. The night sky was clear, empty of clouds and haze. Though it was late, I wasn't ready to return home.

I pulled another arrow out of the quiver, turned, and released it toward the targets. The darkness concealed whether I'd hit the center, but the soft crunch of hay told me I'd hit my mark.

Eight

When my phone rang, I expected the light from Betty's tank but not the blinding daylight of the sun streaming through my bedroom window. I groaned and slapped the bedside table. The phone trilled in an obnoxiously persistent ring—not the same as my alarm.

Oh no. I sat up so fast, tiny blinking stars dotted my vision.

"I slept through the night," I said. After sending a few more arrows into the darkness, I'd locked up the shed shop and called Bella to reinstate our plans for midnight. She agreed to be on the lookout at the Jensen Estate while I slipped into the cracked window.

My phone lit up again, and the vibration sent it sliding off the nightstand and onto the carpet, where the ringing was muffled. Mama had given me Saturdays off during the spring under Grandpa Owl's insistence that I needed to go out on Friday nights. So, I knew this call wasn't from work.

"Fox in a henhouse, I'm coming!" I bent over and my hair tumbled down in a waterfall of auburn waves. Hanging upside down over the side of the bed doubled the number of stars glittering in my sight. I rummaged through a fallen blanket and grabbed my phone.

Folklore Falls P...

The narrow screen cut the name of the caller off. I slid right to answer because I couldn't stand another second of the blaring ring.

"Hello?"

"Ms. Cameron," a voice with a frog in its throat said. "It's Sheriff Max down at the Folklore Falls Police—"

"I know who you are, Max," I said. I struggled to pull myself back to sitting. "Why so formal?"

"Time's up, missy," he said. "I'm sorry, but it's no more Mister Nice Sheriff. I gave you options, and you didn't bother to let me know, so I chose for you."

Crap. I didn't have time to clean up trash or repaint the lines along the highway. But it could be worse. My hair tangled as I twisted it around my fingers and pulled a chunk of locks taut across my face like a mustache.

"You better get on down here."

"I'm starting now?" I asked, as I pulled the phone back to squint at the time and see my mustachioed reflection on the screen.

"What can I say?" Sheriff Max spoke in his lazy voice that almost lulled me back to sleep. "Officer Notting likes to be prompt."

My back stiffened, and my whole body went rigid, sitting in the best posture I'd ever had.

"Officer…" My voice trailed off. I thought nightmares ended when you woke up. "Is this a joke?"

"If I were you, I'd hurry my rear end down here. The sooner you help him find this thief, the sooner you can get back to practicing at the range," Sheriff Max said. "I'd like to hold another archery tournament this summer, and my money's on you. You could take the title away from Brett Jensen."

The thought of wiping the perpetual smug look from the Jensen family's youngest son's face made me smile. Brett was the epitome of entitled jerkhood, like he was forever stuck in the frat house he'd just graduated out of. But he was damn good with a bow and arrow.

"Can practicing be my community service?" I asked, trying to sway him from finalizing this punishment.

"No can do." he sighed. "You're a great resource for the officer's investigation. Who else knows everybody as well as you do?"

I leaned forward and dropped my face into the fluff of my bed's comforter. Who knew my love for Folklore Falls would come back to bite me in the butt?

Sheriff Max seethed. "He's waiting, and he doesn't look too happy. Oh, and Lox, I may have fibbed a bit and told him that assisting me is your part-time job. I don't think he'd take too well to knowing that you have a record."

With that, the sheriff ended the call, and I screamed into the blanket. Hanging around Gideon would suck, but it was the endlessness of it all that horrified me. I couldn't get away from him until we found the thief, but, of course, I could never let him find the thief, either.

The circular cycle reminded me of the Culp's ring as it clamped down and threatened to doom me.

My phone beeped a reminder and I slid up to open a text.

Bella: *Good thing I called you last night before I left. You slept through my call I'm assuming? Or did the dream of Officer Naughty in a towel come true?*

I shot a text back with a long-winded apology and a note about how I regretted sharing my dream with her. Though she'd mixed up Gideon and I's real-life meeting with my nightmare that he'd discovered the truth and arrested me.

I needed to tread into this investigation carefully. Very carefully.

Exactly four people occupied the one-celled police station, including me, Sheriff Max, Gideon, and Falstaff—behind bars. Though I didn't want to smell his whiskey-soaked beard while he enjoyed his Saturday morning sober up, I wanted to trade places with him because my locks and bars came with a sneer and coffee breath.

"I'd hoped you'd dress more professional," Gideon said with a judgmental peak to his eyebrows. His dark eyes raked over my hoodie and jeans as he straightened and yanked his keys from his pocket.

Sheriff Max smiled from behind a mountain of paperwork that probably dated back to my high school years. The waggle of his eyebrows made me grimace. The sheriff had clearly misunderstood the lingering gaze between Officer Notting and me. *Did Grandpa Owl put you up to this?*

The sheriff whistled happily to himself while I followed Gideon out the door with a storm cloud over my head. I'd given in to my fate and planned to come up with an answer along the way. While I couldn't bring myself to blame anyone else for my crimes, I could throw Gideon off my scent—maybe even on a wild goose chase. All I needed to do was find the dagger, sell it to a museum, and I'd have enough cash to spread to the rest of the residents who'd lost their jobs. Maybe I'd hang up my sneaky shoes, the ones with the quiet soles that bent with the arch of my foot, and retire this life of crime for good.

But only psychopaths hang up their shoes.

Gideon opened the passenger side door, then marched for the driver's side. The gentlemanly gesture caught me off guard, but not for long. It wasn't classy so much as a rule of society, and Gideon was nothing if not Mr. Rules.

"So, what's on the agenda?" I popped open the glove box to see if there was anything interesting, like a gun or a pack of gum. I leaned back as Gideon reached across my lap and slammed it shut with a glare beneath angled brows. "You already harassed an innocent housekeeper, so I'm guessing waterboarding a retiree?"

"I wasn't happy when I heard *you* were the sheriff's assistant, either," he said, as he shifted the car in reverse. We backed into a cloud of dirt from his too-fast reversal and clunked over the edge of the paved road as we pulled onto the highway.

"I told you I'm busy with my jobs." I wanted to reinforce Sheriff Max's lie since it kept me off Gideon's radar as someone incapable of breaking the law.

"You know something, and it's inappropriate for you to be keeping it from this investigation."

Okay, so I'm not off his radar. I had hoped he was bad at his job.

"I got wind of a pawn shop just outside city limits," he said. "First order of business is to check their records, cameras, and their list of sellers."

The gentle gnawing of my bottom lip slipped into a bite. I swallowed blood and forced a smile as he glanced my way. The last place I wanted to go was Pop's Pawnshop. Johnny had his ways of concealing his law-avoiding sellers, AKA me, but we'd never gone up against a real investigator before. Sheriff Max spent all of ten minutes going over Johnny's records before throwing in the towel and heading to Fryer Tuck's for lunch.

"You're right," I said, hurrying to think of a plan. "I have a secret."

Gideon side-eyed me. His ruffled, unkempt hair didn't look like that of a dutiful cop's style. He dared to release one hand from ten and two and rake his fingers through his hair. It pushed the waves from his face, and I snapped my gaze away before it turned into a stare.

"I'm waiting." He expected a confession.

The minute he opened his mouth, any slight attraction I might have felt for him dissipated.

"My grandfather has information." *Not a lie.* Grandpa Owl knew everything about everyone except me. The thought sent a weird twinge in my chest, but I chalked it up to another bout of heartburn from my rushed breakfast of ketchup on eggs.

"Hmm," he grunted. "I appreciate the admission. We'll stop at Sherwood's on our way back from the pawnshop."

Son of a biscuit with all the salty gravy. The worst part of visiting Pops would be Johnny's harassment.

I stalked into the pawnshop after Gideon. He only held the door open for ladies when he wasn't in a hurry, apparently.

Johnny greeted us with wide eyes and a wry smile. "How can I help?" His voice carried a tune of amusement as his eyes shifted between me and Gideon.

"I'm Officer Notting, and this is the sheriff's assistant, Ms. Cameron," Gideon said with a flash of his badge. "We're investigating grand larceny and need to go over your books. I assume you keep a record of sellers and items as is expected by law?"

"You assume right," Johnny said. His smirk didn't waver as he whipped a folder out from behind the display case. He balanced his elbows on the glass case and plopped his chin into his open palms.

Gideon sniffed and flipped through the records.

"An investigation, huh?" Johnny peaked his eyebrows.

I rolled my eyes toward the folder, then back at Johnny. He glanced at the cop, then gave me a wink.

"You don't have any repeat sellers?" Gideon asked, incredulous. "I find that hard to believe with your shop sandwiched between two small towns."

"We get a lot of tourists out here." Johnny winked. "Isn't that right, Ms. Cameron?"

I only glared at him. It felt like I stood on the edge of a cliff while I waited. But not Folklore Falls—a rocky, sharp cliff where you couldn't see the bottom.

"Ms. Cameron knows because she likes to date people from out of town." Johnny wiggled his eyebrows up and down. "Isn't that right? Your type is the tall darks with, oh, what did you say?" He snapped his fingers. "Scars!" Johnny pointed at me with two finger guns, and I almost lunged across the case and took him down with the curtain behind him.

Johnny stood as Gideon slapped the record book shut, and I let out a quiet breath. Johnny's *creative* notes kept my name clear. For now.

"I wasn't aware of that." Gideon glanced at me in the stiff-necked way only he could move. "But neither this conversation nor the records are useful for our current investigation. Do you have a camera on the premises?"

"He likes it on video," Johnny said with a nod at me. The joke swooped right over Gideon's head and landed on me with heated cheeks. I wasn't embarrassed, just pissed. Sometimes Johnny's confidence in our little operation went overboard, and I swore he'd flown too close to the sun this time. I scrunched my nose and shook my fist at him when the cop turned around.

"You have videos of your exchanges?" Gideon confirmed.

"All kinds of exchanges," he said, still keeping his eyes on me. I rubbed my palm over my face. As much as I liked our friendship,

Johnny deserved a sock in the throat. Since I wasn't the punching type, I'd wait to challenge him to a game of darts at the tavern or convince him to join the archery tournament and then wipe the range with his ass in front of the whole town to teach him a lesson.

Johnny returned from the back with a laptop of the live feed. It showed dozens of different customers. He'd doctored it to show hundreds more from past years to look as though they'd sold items here recently.

"It's too difficult to see what they're carrying in these," Gideon said.

"I'm sorry, Officer Naughty," Johnny said. "It's hard keeping up with the latest technology."

"Notting." Gideon's voice carried a touch of irritation. "Like Nottingham. The city." His clipped way of speaking was a pleasant contrast to Johnny's exaggerated pitch and theatrical way of saying everything.

Gideon was no nonsense. Normally, I wouldn't like the lack of personality, but it served me well here. He didn't want to waste time, which meant we'd be free of Johnny's harassment and moving onto Grandpa Owl's tales of Falstaff soon. That would keep Gideon busy while I hatched something to distract him with for the evening.

"Do you have any videos from further back?" Gideon asked. "Anything clearer?"

"I can see some of them," I piped up and stepped forward. I pointed to the shape of the item in a woman's hands. "That's a lamp. You can tell by the bulbous shape. And he's likely carrying jewelry because there's a shine."

Gideon almost smiled. I could only tell by the way the sword-shaped scar folded into the smile line at the edge of his mouth. "You're right."

We watched almost an hour of video feed while Johnny helped customers. Gideon eyed everyone that came in with cartoonishly pointed eyebrows that only relaxed when he thanked me for identifying objects.

Once we were back in the car, I took a deep breath of the fresh air blowing through the vents. I'd survived the first hurdle. Maybe this wouldn't be so bad.

Gideon had even relaxed a little since I told him my 'secret' about Grandpa Owl. Maybe he trusted me. I needed to hold on to that until I could find and snag the dagger, then send the cop on his merry way chasing a nonexistent tourist out of town.

After a few minutes of silence, Gideon glanced at me.

"Did he call me naughty?" he asked with a thumb over his shoulder to point in the general direction of the pawnshop.

The release of tension burst, and I couldn't help but laugh.

"That's a new look for Oscar the Grouch," I said.

"I know I come across as grumpy, but I don't mean to be rude," he said. The gentle tone threw me for a loop. I looked at him and noticed the wrinkles at the corners of his eyes had softened. He glanced at me, then back to the road.

"Well, you could have fooled me," I said, referring to the attitude—one that I preferred to avoid. I stared at the road in front of us until the town came into view. From a distance, the most noticeable building was Sherwood Bed and Breakfast since it stood taller than the diner, bookstore, laundromat, and the empty buildings where the shuttered businesses once were.

"I doubt that," he said.

I furrowed my brows and shifted my gaze to him again.

Gideon flicked on the blinker and eased the car into the B and B parking lot before meeting my gaze with a glance. "You're observant." He nodded. "It's a good skill to have, especially if you ever decide to go for a promotion at the station."

The suggestion of me becoming a cop made me want to shrivel. I'd never sit around with piles of paperwork like Sheriff Max or risk accusing innocent people like Gideon. So, why did I like the compliment?

We left the car and hopped up Sherwood's front steps. Grandpa Owl wasn't in his chair, which meant he either needed a nap or Mama needed his help inside. Gideon reached for the door and waved for me to enter.

"Plus," he said, "you're passionate about taking care of the town's people. That's important."

The bell on the front door jingled, and I stepped inside, feeling the heat of Gideon's body as I passed. I might observe visual cues and my surroundings—I had to, as a thief, but Gideon was the one who listened carefully. And he remembered what I cared about.

Nine

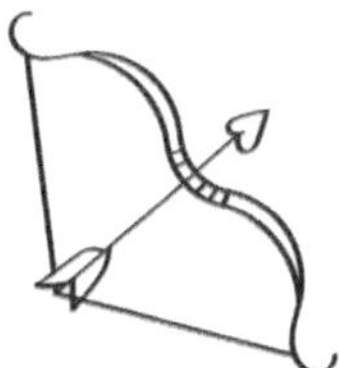

Who knew Gideon and Grandpa would become best buddies? At least, that was how it felt to the third wheel—AKA me.

Their chairs even rocked at the same rhythm, both squeaking against Sherwood porch's wooden planks. The cop relaxed just enough to deep dive into everything Grandpa Owl knew about the thefts in Folklore Falls, which was enough to keep Gideon interested. It helped that Grandpa Owl told the most boring of facts with a flair and storyteller's magic that captivated both of us. Even me, who had already lived the stories of skirting security cameras, taming watchdogs, and moving like an invisible force amongst the elite, wanted more of Grandpa Owl's take on it.

I sat with my back against the fence that circled the porch's edges. The carved slats were angled for flourish, which added to Sherwood's charm and brought out the history of the people who built the town of Folklore Falls hundreds of years ago. Pretty enough, but not comfortable against my spine. I stood and paced the length of the porch, stopping long enough to smile at the couple on their second honeymoon as they exited.

"Yeah, it's fascinating, really," Grandpa Owl said, as he wrapped up the story. He leaned over the arm of the rocking chair and picked up his current sewing project, new tablecloths for the B and B's dining room. "This thief is as good as the fox who keeps snagging our baby chicks. He's like a ghost."

"Dogs bark at ghosts," Gideon said. I couldn't tell if it was a joke or not, but the fact that he almost admitted he believed in the supernatural gave me hope for the cop yet. Maybe he wasn't as boring as his title would have me believe. Or it could just be Grandpa Owl's charm. My gramps brought out the whimsical in everyone. "So, he risked a bite from a trained attack dog but stole nothing? What makes you think that break-in is related to our thief?"

"All the signs matched," Grandpa Owl said. His tongue pressed against the side of his lips as he focused on threading an embroidery string through the eye of a needle.

Signs? I paused my pacing. What signs did I leave behind?

"He seems to leave a pattern."

Gideon nodded and flipped a page in his mini spiral-bound notepad. He licked his fingers and flipped again, settling on a half-empty page. "He hits vacationers' homes. I'm assuming because they're empty, easy targets. He could be lazy."

Hey! I'm not lazy. I'm smart. Besides, I only stole from certain vacationers—the ones who treated the residents with judgment or took advantage of our kindness. If he wanted to track patterns, maybe he should look at who I stole from.

"Yes," Grandpa Owl said. "He also repeats targets. He's nabbed a few things from the Hills' home three times now."

Of course I did. Mrs. Hill hit-and-run a resident's car, screamed at Fryer Tuck, and successfully sued Bones for putting her picture up at the bar, even though *everybody* who gets drunk enough to puke gets a mugshot on the wall at Knight's Tavern. It was the eighth wonder of the world that an elite vacationer would even set foot in the tavern, much less drink the cheap whiskey.

The pencil scratched against Gideon's notepad as he scribbled. I peered over his shoulder when I casually paced by. Each word was capitalized, and his handwriting was boxy and bold—about as lacking in a flourish as his personality.

Repeat offender. Interview with the Hills. Check for evidence surrounding the missing statue.

My breath caught in my throat as I saw the word 'missing,' then the slice of hope crashed with the following word. The rollercoaster of emotions continued when Gideon added one more note.

Is the missing statue related to the missing dagger?

He believed me? My heart sped. Even Mama claimed the legend wasn't real and the dagger didn't exist. But I'd seen it, and I'd heard the rumors among the vacationers. *Someone* had found it and taken it.

"Can you tell me anything about the legend from around town?" Gideon asked. "If you could give me the SparkNotes version, I'd appreciate it. I—" He glanced up at me, and I shifted from my sneaky position behind him and back toward the fence around the porch. "We need to head over to the Hills' place ASAP."

We? Right, I was Sheriff Max's assistant. Just when I thought I'd distracted the cop enough to forget about my 'job.'

Grandpa Owl rested the embroidery hoop on his lap and waved the needle around as he spoke. He started with a long sigh and the flash of a smile. Grandpa loved the legend almost as much as I did. But to him, it was just another fun story to tell.

"Six hundred years ago, Grayson Baird lived both here and Scotland. It is said he traveled back and forth through the faery realm. Eventually, he fell for a faery who was a servant in Oberon and Titiana's court. She was only allowed to leave with Grayson if he could prove he could make his world as enchanting as the faery realm. Titiana gifted him a dagger, and he spent sixty-seven years carving the falls we have today."

"The Shakespeare characters?" Gideon asked. I didn't like that he interrupted Grandpa Owl's smooth, lilting voice, but I smiled at the question. I didn't expect a guy like Gideon to know anything about Shakespeare, much less remember the names of the fairies in *A Midsummer Night's Dream*. Color me impressed.

"They're not just Shakespeare's creations," I said.

"In any case," Grandpa Owl continued. "They eventually released the faery from her service for the faery king and queen, and she married Grayson at the falls. The history of the land shows that Folk-lore River did drastically change into an unnatural formation that led to the falls. And the storms we have are unparalleled. People say its from the faery realm since the lightning is so dangerously precise. It's unexplainable."

"It's not unexplainable, it was Baird," I said. I knew I sounded like a child defending Santa Claus or the Tooth Fairy, but I'd seen the dang dagger, and after years of stealing diamonds, I knew exactly what the blade was made from.

Gideon shot me a raised eyebrow, and I looked away. Who cared what the jerk thought of me? I *never* cared that people teased me for defending the legend. Not once.

"Little Robin saw the dagger," Grandpa Owl said. As much as I lied about other things, this one was true, and he believed it. Though Grandpa Owl insisted the person who invented the story placed the dagger in the rock, rather than the faery herself, Ellery. She'd embedded it in the rock after Grayson died and she returned to the faery realm. Without that dagger, our town wouldn't have existed since the area didn't have access to fresh water before the change in Folklore River.

Gideon laughed, thinking Grandpa Owl's statement was a joke. The sword-shaped scar vanished into his smile lines and was replaced with nearby dimples that I hadn't noticed before now. Had he never laughed? I'd only known him for a few days, but when you want to get away from someone and you're forced to help them, every hour feels like a week.

"Little Robin?" he asked.

"It's just a nickname," I said. "I thought we were going." I pointed toward the steps and made my way to the edge of the porch. "Evidence, right?"

He stood and thanked my grandfather.

"You look like you need a good day off. Will you be around for the Jensen's Grand Reopening Gala?" Grandpa Owl asked. His gaze flickered to me, and I snapped my head away to stare at the trees on the edge of Sherwood Forest.

"Not if I catch the thief before then," Gideon said. "If I take too long solving this, I'll be stuck here on desk duty forever." He made an odd sound from the base of his throat. "But I'll admit, I do need a better balance between work and life. I've been told that before."

I glanced back and waved for Gideon to follow me as I took a step off the porch.

"Well, Loxley has finally come around to attending the event, and you two would look good together."

I gritted my teeth and shot Grandpa Owl a frown. I'd vehemently protested the event before my investigation unearthed clues that pointed to the Jensens. Based on the gossip and Brett Jensen's tendency to hang around town longer than most of the vacationers, they were the most likely suspects. Now, I wouldn't miss the Gala for the world. It was the perfect opportunity to move around the Jensen Estate without suspicion.

Gideon glanced between us and only shrugged. "I plan to be gone before the next two weeks."

The moment we left Grandpa Owl's presence, Gideon resumed his fast-paced, aggressive hunt for… me. He drove exactly the speed limit but jumped out of the car, marched as if we were in a race, and pounded on the Hills' front door.

"I didn't realize it was already four in the afternoon," he grumbled.

Time wasted? Achievement unlocked. Gideon thought my secret about Grandpa Owl's information was his knowledge of Falstaff's Friday binge drinking. I'd shrugged and pretended to think that the illegal activity interested the cop. And by that time, Grandpa Owl had already sucked Gideon in with his stories. Or maybe Gideon liked the stories. I couldn't tell, but my grandfather had slowed the cop, both calming and captivating him.

Once inside, Mrs. Hill eyed me. She'd returned when the security camera revealed the mantel was empty of the statue. The way I'd avoided that camera was a trick I was proud of.

"You said you're working for Sheriff Max now?" she asked. Her doctored skin pinched oddly around her eyes. "I thought you worked over at that old motel."

"It's a bed-and-breakfast," I corrected with a quick, tight-lipped smile. "And we prefer historical rather than old."

Mrs. Hill arched her eyebrow, and it surprised me that part of her face could move. She had enough surgery to cover her own 'historical' features.

"And you're the only one with access to the security cameras, but you say they show nothing?" Gideon asked.

"That's right," Mrs. Hill said. She twisted her face into something of a smile that crashed and burned after the cop's next statement.

"Thieves aren't invisible, Mrs. Hill," he said. "I'd like to see the videos myself, and just so you're aware, I don't take kindly to insurance fraud."

It was my turn to raise my eyebrows. Once again, Gideon flipped my understanding of him upside down. Maybe he didn't unjustly accuse only housekeepers and bed-and-breakfast maids. Maybe he unjustly accused everyone. His rudeness was one of equality. I appreciated he suspected the rich and fancy as much as he did the rest of us.

One Oscar the Grouch look from Gideon, and Mrs. Hill left us alone in the study with the computer that stored the security videos.

Gideon squinted at the screen, and I wondered if he needed glasses. Thick black frames would look smart on his face and might even clean up the messy look caused by overgrown waves that hung over one eyebrow.

He paused the video and leaned across me to reach the tasseled tie that kept the curtains open. A rush of sandalwood and mint from the gum he always chewed brought me back to our first awkward, yet memorable meeting at the B and B. Except now he was wearing pants.

"Excuse me," I said, as I came back to the present and realized he'd nearly clocked me in the nose with his elbow. "Do they not teach manners in the city?"

The curtain fell closed, encompassing the room in darkness other than the glow from the computer screen. Gideon froze with his arm halfway pulled back. Apparently, people rarely spoke to him in that tone of voice. His look of shock was almost cute. I liked the way his eyebrows ticked in confusion, then curved into an apologetic expression.

But he didn't say sorry. Instead, Gideon straightened and blew a puff of air from his nose. He held my gaze for a moment before shaking his head and returning his attention to the screen.

"What? You almost whacked me in the face," I said, feeling an odd need to defend myself. Why did I want to explain my actions to him? He didn't matter. He was an outsider who'd return to the city soon, and he'd be nothing more than a distant, bad memory.

"Nothing," he said. He tapped the space bar on the keyboard to resume the video.

I tapped it to pause again and looked at him. "No, you laughed at me." *Fox in a henhouse, Loxley, who cares?* But I did, and my common sense wasn't going to talk me out of getting an answer from him.

"I didn't laugh."

"Okay, you snorted."

Gideon glanced at me with an odd smirk, and it only fueled my fire. Fire unrelated to my acid reflux, thankfully. Though my plain peanut butter sandwich for lunch was probably the only reason my heart wasn't burning along with my attitude right now.

"You just surprise me is all," he said. He tapped the keyboard again to play the video.

Oh, you have no idea. I tapped the pause.

"I take it nobody has ever stood up to the grumpy old cop before?"

Gideon lifted his hand, but instead of landing his finger on the space bar, he curled his fist and dropped it on the desk before looking at me again.

"You know what? No," he said. "I'm not the friendliest person, and I don't trust easily. People sense that and often leave me alone. So, why do I feel like you're a tick burrowing under my skin all the time?"

My jaw dropped. "Excuse me?" I repeated with all the animosity and none of the shock from before. "I don't have to help you." *Lie.*

"I thought this was your job."

"I have other... investigations," I said. *Not entirely untrue.* I had an investigation of my own, including a countdown—find the dagger before the vacationers come for the summer. "Besides, the sooner you leave, the better. Right?" *True. One hundred percent true.* I definitely didn't want him hanging around longer than he needed. Definitely.

"That's right," he said. "Let's solve this, so I can leave, and you can get back to your other investigations."

My investigations. *Wait. That's it!* I was observant, sneaky, and, well, a criminal. But I didn't have the professional training of an investigator like Mr. Naughty—Notting—here. If I led him to believe he was trailing the thief when he was actually following the same clues I had for finding the dagger, he could lead me right to it.

"Agreed," I said. "And you can get rid of this tick." I turned and tapped the space bar. The video rolled, showing scans of the front yard, the doors, the living room, including the mantel, and the garage with the Corvette.

"Loyalty isn't a bad thing," he said.

I scoffed but didn't break my gaze on the screen to look at him and give him the satisfaction of my attention. "Ticks suck blood and spread disease."

"I'm bad with words," he said. "I'm not like your grandfather that way. I just meant you've been here, with this investigation and me, since I arrived in Folklore Falls. But you also… I don't know." He shrugged, and I caught the movement out of the corner of my eye. "You bite."

The word must have triggered my subconscious. I realized I was gnawing on my bottom lip.

"And you're a grump," I said, a weak attempt at a comeback that wasn't even necessary.

"I don't deny it," he said, his eyes burning holes in the side of my face. Why was he staring at me? We'd come here to watch the video, not each other.

He had an attitude, and I had a temper. Maybe Gideon and I were more alike than I wanted to admit.

But of course, he didn't have the animosity for me I had for him. He didn't know who I really was.

"Look," I said, pointing at the screen.

Gideon followed my gaze, and I traced the thin line in the video. Since I couldn't reach this camera to shift where it viewed, I'd used an arrow and fishing wire to tack onto the camera. Once the arrow landed on the other side, I pulled it down, winding the wire around the neck of the camera, then I'd tugged it to face down. Only the shadow of the ghost could be seen cast across the floor as I marched up to the mantel and took the ugly naked statue that paid for another month of insulin for the woman down the street from me.

"It's fishing wire," I said.

Gideon leaned forward and squinted. "Huh. It is."

I tread a thin line between getting caught and leading him to my investigation.

He looked at me and nodded. "Observant."

The compliment left my whole body warm. And since the curtain blocked the afternoon sun, I needed a little warmth.

I used to say I was better off alone. Just me and Betty the Betta, and the help from Bella and Johnny, of course.

But partners sounded pretty good.

A flutter of excitement beat in my chest. I'd never considered having someone else alongside me on the hunt for the dagger, and though Gideon didn't know it, we'd just become partners in two separate investigations.

Partnership turned into day after day of interviews with the so-called victims, taking notes and pictures of my past break-in locations, and enough coffee to wire us both for another week. Not everyone we spoke with had a familiar face. I'd stolen from plenty from the town's elite visitors, but some of them either misplaced their jewelry or had a run-in with thieves while at their *other* homes or on their worldwide trips.

I took another swig from the paper coffee cup to find it empty. It tipped when I dropped my arm back on the table. The small police station boasted a grand total of one desk—Sheriff Max's, one cell, a storage closet that held lost and found items as well as evidence in ongoing investigations, and one round table. We'd cleared off the sheriff's piles of procrastinated paperwork and taken over the table for the day.

Gideon raked his fingers through his hair and sighed. He leaned back in the chair, giving me a full view of the corded muscles on his forearm and the curve of his bicep.

The constant lying exhausted me, but having him as a partner had its perks too. Visual perks.

"Are you as bored as I am?" I asked, as I balanced my head on my palm and tapped one finger against my cheek.

When he shook his head, hair fell into his face. Much to my disappointment, he didn't lift his arm and brush the hair back again.

"I think the word you're looking for is tedious," he said. He glanced from the mountain of notes and to me. The pinch of his thick, dark eyebrows looked aggressive, but I'd gotten used to it over the past week. "And some of us care about the details."

"Oh, I'm good with details." I sat up, straightening. With my veins full of caffeine, I readied to defend my honor. To Gideon, I was a mildly helpful assistant with a knack for observation and an obsession with an old folklore. I couldn't share the skilled side of me without risking exposure. "I can read people. Like I can tell that you didn't believe Mr. Hoffman when he said his Tom Ford cuff links were taken after he arrived in Folklore Falls."

Gideon made a sound between a laugh and a scoff. "Because they weren't. He'd only been in town for two hours when he called to report them missing, and it so happened to line up with when Sheriff Max spoke to the news reporter about the investigation on TV. Mr. Hoffman was looking to blame someone, but since he took a plane and the closest airport is three hours away, we know nobody from here could have stolen those cuff links."

I folded my arms and smirked. "So, why are you still going over his notes if you know that? I thought we were going to close his claim and be done for the night."

He scratched at his eyebrow and scraped his teeth over his bottom lip before landing his gaze back on me. "I just wanted to determine a good, solid lead before this week ends." His throat bobbed with a swallow.

My stomach twisted, and I pressed my lips together to ensure that I wouldn't accidentally say "I'm sorry" out loud. Gideon was a good guy, he wanted to help others. And he could do that by inadvertently helping me find the dagger. But I didn't love the idea of manipulating the person who considered me his partner.

We needed a break.

Neither of us had the time for it, but staring at the same notes wouldn't get us any more answers. The words melted into one another and looked like an unsolvable puzzle after too many hours of staring. I needed the big name players in town for him to question—the Evanses, Tamsens, and Jensens. Scrubbing over our current notes wouldn't make them arrive here any faster.

"What about the Franklin family's confession? Isn't that a lead?" I knew it wasn't much, but at least it was something. Maybe Gideon would relax, and if I could get him to do that, I could move mountains. The guy was wound tighter than a bowstring. Relax first, dagger second. Eventually, I'd get him to realize that helping people meant locating that piece of history and donating the money—not worrying about cuff links and watches.

"We have no reason to believe that Jimmy Franklin stole the other items just because he was lying about his affair," he said, shuffling the papers around as if that would reveal new evidence.

"And he stole his mistress's wedding ring," I added.

"I wouldn't call that so much a theft as him wanting to hide that she's also married so his wife wouldn't contact the other woman's husband. The guy's a coward, he doesn't want to get beat up." He reached for his coffee cup and downed the last sip of the beverage that had gone cold hours ago.

I tilted my head back and forth but was forced to agree. "True. But what if Jimmy has a lot of girlfriends, and he's taking all their jewelry? And the men's items that are gone could be due to his jealousy." Mr. Franklin hiked the falls several times last summer, so he was still on *my* list of suspects, even if he didn't relate to the investigation anymore. But the affair threw a wrench in the plan and convinced Gideon they weren't involved. I needed to get one more interview with the Franklins and add a couple of questions of my own.

Gideon arched an eyebrow. It was a new look for him.

"What?" I shrugged.

"I thought you could read people."

"I can."

He licked his lips and set the empty cup down. "Then, you know the guy's too much of a wimp to even attempt what you suggested."

"I still think he could be involved with more thefts. He's proven he has the ability to steal. He hid his mistress's wedding ring for weeks." And maybe the dagger. Jimmy Franklin was about as shady as they came. I was willing to bet he had a few other crimes up his sleeve.

Gideon sighed.

"One more interview with the Franklins," I proposed.

He shook his head. "I have a schedule that I plan to keep, and they're not on it anymore."

"Fine." I scooted the chair back and stood. "We both need a break from these notes, but we can't talk with anyone tonight. So, how about a bet?"

He folded his arms and leaned back in the chair. A little shudder of excitement rippled through me as I held his full attention. But it was the thought of introducing Gideon to my real life that delighted me. He wouldn't fit in, not by a long shot. It was the slice of honesty, the thought of sharing a piece of myself with this new partner of mine that I wanted.

"We take the rest of the night off and go to Knight's Tavern." I scooped up my paper cup. "If you win at darts, we'll forget Jimmy Franklin and you have to promise to stop going over useless notes. But if I win, we interview them again and I'm betting we'll find *something*."

Gideon shook his head, but his smile betrayed him. It wasn't big, and appeared on rare occasions, but the bit of happiness reached his eyes with wrinkles in the corners.

"And don't call it a waste of time." I pointed at him. "Clearing your head is better than staring at the same pages."

He nodded and stood. "It's a bet."

The gasp that slipped from my mouth surprised both of us. I didn't expect him to agree so easily.

"What?" He mirrored my shrug from earlier. It looked awkward on his broad shoulders. Gideon didn't know how to be casual, so the gesture split him like a sky between a storm when half was blue and the other half was covered in dark clouds. I loved those days. "Didn't see that coming? Can't you read me? I need a work-life balance, and this would be a good opportunity to practice that."

I smirked and lofted the cup in the air. Though it wasn't a bow and arrow, the aim was similar. The cup landed in the trash can by Sheriff Max's desk.

"I'm sensing that you're already ready to accept defeat," I said.

Gideon didn't give me the satisfaction of a response. He simply swiveled on his heels and headed for the door. If I didn't catch the smirk on his face before he turned, I might consider the lack of response rude. Instead, I recognized the cop's attempt at playfulness. He still had a long way to go for that work-life balance, though, considering the whole bet centered around the investigation.

Music blared from the tavern as we approached. Stars glittered above us, visible now that most of the town had shut down for the night. Only Sherwood Bed and Breakfast and Knight's still had lights on. In the distance, floodlights from Jensen Resort's tennis courts and pool areas lit up the sky. But here, in the heart of the town, the velvet blanket of blackness above us was untouched by the glare of city lights.

Katrina nearly tackled me with a hug as we entered. Every table and bar stool was taken. Bones shouted a greeting from behind the bar. He raised a glass of whiskey with his hello and then took a swig directly from the bottle.

"Don't worry," Katrina's words slurred. "That's his own personal bottle. Not the s-same one he pours shots from."

"Uh-huh." I nodded and glanced at Gideon. He stood as stiff as a statue, his hands in his pockets and jaw clenched. The song "Sweet Home Alabama" came on, and while half the ladies in the bar cheered, a loud booing cut through them.

Bella sat in the corner with her black boots perched on the edge of a pool table. She rested her arms over a pool cue and took a large breath to shout another boo.

I nodded toward the bar. "We have to get our darts from Bones and get in line for a game."

Gideon followed as we zigzagged through the tables and bodies and an older couple line dancing. The bounce of Katrina's steps created a pathway for us in the chaos. People moved out of her way as if she were a celebrity because everyone knew if they so much as looked at the redhead wrong, Bones would challenge them to a duel.

"Shot?" Bones asked, pointing to us with his personal bottle.

Gideon shook his head, but Bones whipped out two small glasses. He grabbed a second bottle of Wild Turkey, filled the shot glasses, and took another swig from his bottle, all without spilling a drop.

"Put it on my tab," I said.

"If you take both, maybe I'll have a chance at this bet," Gideon shouted over a round of raucous laughter from a group by the pool tables. He stood close enough for his body heat to warm my back. The minty smell of his breath would soon be replaced with the spice of whiskey. The dagger and the townspeople were important, but tonight was all about getting Gideon Notting to relax.

"Not happening." I shoved a shot into his hands. "I stacked the bet so I could win."

"You forget I have practiced aim too," he said.

I raised my eyebrows. My mind went somewhere else, but Gideon quickly snapped me back to a less dirty reality with his mention of going to the shooting range regularly—the bullet kind rather than bows and arrows.

"Didn't you just admit you don't have a chance?" I threw back the shot and felt the liquid warm me all the way down.

"I'm testing your claim to read people." The whiskey in his glass swirled as he lifted it, then dropped his arm from his face without taking it.

"Sure." I nodded and rolled my eyes toward the shot. "So, when are we scheduling the interview?"

Gideon smirked and shook his head. "What's that saying? Pride goes before..." he pursed his lips. Taking him away from his work already served to pull him from his shell. Knight's had a way of doing that to people. Even the elite vacationers who dared step through the doors found themselves racking up a bill, playing games, and getting their photographs posted on the wall.

"How's that work-life balance going?" I scooted back to a barstool that a woman had abandoned for a game of pool.

Gideon glanced down at his full glass of whiskey and nodded. "Better."

"I told you Knight's is fun." I gestured around the room and reached for my regular beer Bones plopped on the bartop.

"Fun isn't usually in my vocabulary." He scratched at the scar with his free hand. Another stool opened up, and I patted the seat with my palm.

"And why is that?" I clinked the top of my beer bottle against his glass as he took a seat beside me.

Gideon's gaze swept over the room and landed on me. He lifted the shot and threw it back with one gulp. When he dropped the empty glass back on the bartop, Bones whooped and took a celebratory swig from his personal bottle.

"Fun and protecting people don't usually go hand in hand," he said. "But I've been told before that I need to loosen up." Gideon's gaze shifted behind me, and he seemed to stare at nothing. The distant look in his eyes sobered me, and I set the beer down. The buzz of conversation, shouts, and laughter faded from my attention. "Someone I cared about used to say life is meant to be enjoyed not just survived."

I nodded, returning the favor of listening carefully. Gideon was a blip on the timeline of my year. He'd be gone before summer was in full swing, and we'd likely never see each other again. So, I intended to leave him with a good impression of Folklore Falls, though that was nothing new for me. Everyone deserved to experience the joy of our small town through the legend, the falls, and the really good whiskey.

"This someone you speak of sounds wise," I said, taking a sip of the grainy beer. "I wholeheartedly agree."

"I can tell." He lifted his chin to gesture toward the room.

"I'm sensing you don't agree with my belief that work itself should be fun too?" I narrowed my eyes, pretending to be 'reading' him like a book.

He twisted his lips and considered this. "It's not that I don't agree. It's that I didn't know it was possible before—"

"You're up." Bones plopped a pile of darts in front of us and pointed to the open board on the wall. The colors of the targets had faded around the outside with hundreds of holes poking into the fiber but the red in the center remained vibrant.

I smiled at Gideon and grabbed the blue darts. "I don't tell stories as well as my grandfather, but I promise I'll make the drive back to the Franklins' a fun part of work with plenty of folklore." I hopped off the stool and led the way to the dartboard. The heat of Gideon's body assured me he followed closely. I glanced back to see the dig had registered and his pinched brows relaxed.

He shook his head. "I don't doubt it, but that's *if* we go back to the Franklin's house."

I waved for him to give me space and positioned myself to throw the first dart. It landed just outside the red target. I swirled around and shot him a smile.

Gideon folded his arms and shifted his feet wider to even his stance. The posture looked stiff, possibly arrogant, but the fact that he'd come here and taken the bet in the first place proved he'd made an attempt to relax.

I threw the next two darts and racked up fifty-six points, better than the average player. From the right, Bella shot me a thumbs up. The effect of the whiskey sunk in and left me feeling warm and wanting to dance.

Gideon stepped up and launched his first dart. It stuck into the outer ring. He shook his head and tried again, only to hit the wall. When he shot me a look, I shrugged and smiled.

"Is it too late to add to the bet?" I twirled one of the darts around until I pointed it toward the older couple on the other side of the bar. "I'd love to see you try to line dance."

He shook his head, letting the hair fall into his face. No wonder he couldn't land a good one with all that dark hair blocking his vision. A thought of raking my fingers through it flashed in my mind.

"Maybe I'm pro at line dancing," he said.

I scrunched my nose. "Nah, it's too fun for Oscar the Grouch."

Without breaking our gaze, Gideon threw the next dart. It wasn't until he sauntered toward the dartboard that I saw the silver flag from last dart covering the red target.

"Are you sandbagging me?" My mouth hung open.

"Beginner's luck?" He shrugged as he walked back.

"Lie." I crossed my arms.

"I never lie," he said. "That was luck."

The next several rounds proved his statement true. Gideon struggled to land the darts anywhere but the outer ring. Some even stuck into the wall next to the dartboard for which he earned mocking laugh from Bella. Rich coming from someone who only held a pool cue to threaten people from nearing her personal bubble rather than actually playing the game. Still, townsfolk loved Bella, because everyone knew her rough exterior had more to do with being unique like the main characters in her favorite books rather than being cold. One step in her bookstore revealed all the warm, fuzzies beneath the ripped clothes and black lipstick.

"Give the poor guy some pointers," Bones said, as he delivered a fresh beer. He nodded at Gideon and gave me a cheeky look. The cold bottle sweat and dripped condensation over my fingers.

"I doubt he'd accept if I offered," I said, taking a drink. Another dart whiffed as Gideon launched it into the wall.

He swept his gaze over me as he walked to the dartboard. "As much as I'd like a chance to hear more folklore, I'd appreciate a win."

"Is that a yes?" I asked.

When he didn't respond, I handed Katrina my beer and positioned myself to throw again. But this time, I explained my stance and where I focused my eyes.

Gideon nodded, listening carefully as he always did. On his turn, he repeated what I'd said and landed all three darts on the board. Katrina cheered for him and seemed to have forgotten the beer she held was mine. She downed it in two swigs and bounded back to Bones at the bar.

By his next throw, Gideon returned to the bad habit of slouching with both feet side-by-side. I shook my head.

"Best foot forward."

"Like this?" He shuffled to move his right foot in front, but now it looked like he was trying to lunge in a yoga class.

"This isn't in my best interest considering I'm on the Jimmy-Franklin-stole-jewelry train, but I can help. May I?" I stepped up to him and held my hand out under his arm.

"Sure."

Gideon let me adjust his position. I resisted giving the muscles of his forearm a squeeze. The smell of mint lingered even around the spice of whiskey on his breath. He brushed the hair from his face and struggled to shift his foot into the right place. I pressed my palm into his back to straighten his posture.

"Okay, now look there."

"Here?"

I ran my hand over his arm where he pointed and gently pushed it to the right spot. Our height difference forced me to arch my feet to see from his perspective. But I was an archer not a ballerina, and the balance on my tiptoes didn't last. I had to lean into him to keep from falling. My body pressed against his side, and my cheeks burned as he broke his gaze on the dartboard and ran it over me.

When his eyes landed on mine, I forgot where we were. Tonight was about getting Gideon to relax and winning a bet, I didn't factor in a moment like this. His gaze dropped to my mouth, and my chin instinctively tilted up without my permission. The bare distance between our faces closed ever-so-slightly when he dipped his head and opened his mouth to say something.

"I brought you another—oops!" Katrina's voice shattered the tension. I released a breath, and it seemed Gideon did the same. We quickly pulled apart, but the heat of our bodies pressed together made everything else feel cold. A slight shiver ran through me, and the beer felt icy in my hand as Katrina gave it to me.

"Yo," Bella shouted. I glanced over at the pool tables to see her pointing the pool cue between Gideon and me. "Do you two need to get a room or what? I know a place by Sherwood." Her black lips twisted into a wicked smile. Bella had an odd way of expressing her love for all things romantic.

"I didn't mean to interrupt anything." Katrina hiccupped. "Bones!" She turned and shouted toward the bar. "You need to cut me off, I've had too much."

Gideon and I both smiled, letting the tension bubble into laughter. When he fixed his stance again, he let the arrow fly. It landed beside the target, upping his score. He squeezed his hand into a fist and pumped it in front of him.

"Good," I said, "but that was your last one."

He sighed and raked his fingers through his hair, then folded his arms. Both movements exhibited the muscles in his arms that threw my mind off track.

"I guess I'll have to make room in my schedule for a trip to the Franklins' and some folklore." Gideon smiled, and I relished the rare sighting.

Mission to get Gideon to relax, complete. And I'd won the bet.

That was all tonight meant. Nothing else.

Tomorrow we'd return to our regularly scheduled program of tedious paperwork and plenty of interviews that would hopefully lead me closer to Grayson Baird's dagger. For once, I agreed with the cop: we didn't have time for fun.

Eleven

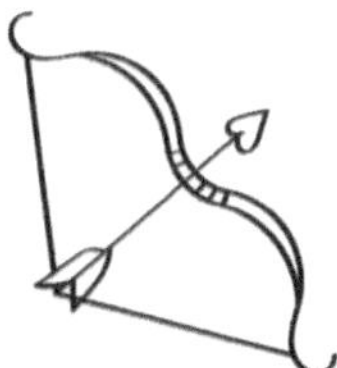

The next Sunday evening, we found ourselves at Fryer Tuck's again to discuss the interview with Jimmy Franklin. This time, Gideon ordered a mountain of fries, which he shared liberally.

I gave the chicken wrap a try since I knew I'd be out all night, clearing the last vacation home from my list. I didn't need a stomach full of grease and food that made me sleepy before breaking into the Evanses and scouting for the dagger. I doubted Mr. and Mrs. Evans had anything to do with the missing artifact since they were both well into their seventies and likely couldn't climb the hike to Folklore Falls anymore, but I needed to rule them out anyway.

"You owe me for being wrong about Jimmy," Gideon said and his lips twitched into a faint smirk. I threw a french fry at him that landed in his lap. He picked it up and set it on a napkin, too much of a clean freak to eat it after it'd touched his pants.

"So, I was wrong." I shrugged. "At least, we can throw that whole page of notes away and not stare at them any longer." I'd ruled out the Franklins after the second interview when it was clear Jimmy was incapable of stealing anything other than another man's wife. His mistress had even come forward and had admitted she let him take her wedding ring.

"True." He nodded, wiping the grease from the fried food off his fingers with a second napkin.

"Am I a bad influence?" I asked. I pointed to the plate of potatoes.

Gideon smiled, and the scar disappeared. Both looked as equally intriguing on his face. The scar suited his gruff demeanor, but he had a heart underneath that made special appearances. I'd found myself wanting to trigger those special appearances.

"Balance is key," he said. "You've got it nailed."

I tilted my head and half-smiled before taking another bite of the chicken wrap.

"You work for the police department, but stay relaxed," he explained. "But not lazy like Sheriff Max."

I laughed. "Relaxed Max, that's definitely him."

Gideon shook his head, but the smile remained. "He's not one who'd ever last at the station I come from, that's for sure."

"I don't think he cares."

"Sometimes I'm envious of that," he said, swallowing another fry. "I care too much."

I set the wrap down. Another customer screamed out her to-go order of seven milkshakes. Fryer Tuck grunted in acknowledgment. He'd let his server go early, and I didn't have to think too hard to guess that it was because of financial struggles. Folklore Fall residents kept the restaurant afloat, but barely. Tuck used to draw in hundreds of families starting at this time of year—families that now opted for the chain restaurant built inside Jensen Resort over the homemade but non-brand-name fries at Tuck's.

"I think what matters is what types of things you care about," I said.

It was his turn to tilt his head. Gideon's confusion came with a slight crease between his brow that wasn't visible when he wore his blue-light glasses.

"Like I care about the people and this town," I said. "They're all my family. I'd do anything for them." I told him about Sara and Billy and Diana, plus Fryer Tuck and the others in the neighborhood that needed help. Of course, I couldn't admit I was the one who helped them—anonymously leaving cash in indiscreet burlap bags by their front doors whenever I pawned a piece of jewelry or snagged a wallet.

Gideon nodded, listening to every story. "You want to protect them?"

"Yes."

"That's why I do what I do," he said. "I want to protect people, but it doesn't always work out the way I hope."

I chewed on my lip and considered a risky play. Was it a play? I wanted to lead him toward the search for the person who took the dagger rather than the town thief, but I couldn't help wondering if he'd help me. If he knew more about the dagger and the legend and how it could help save residents' homes and businesses, would he change his investigation?

"What if you could help the people here another way?" I asked.

His eyebrows ticked up, and he swallowed but didn't pick up another fry. "Is this about the dagger?"

Fox in a henhouse. Was I that transparent? Not a chance. I lied better than a chicken with her eggs, which meant he'd listened more carefully than I'd thought.

I shrugged. "It's stolen, and you're not investigating it."

"It wasn't reported to me."

"Well, I'm reporting it," I said. "And I bet that finding it could help you find the thief."

"You think they're the same person?"

"It's possible," I said, trying not to get too excited that he was considering it. *Partners?* Of course, he could never know who I really was. I needed to remind myself of that. Often. "I could show you where it was taken from. Grayson Baird embedded it into a rock and buried the rock by the falls."

"Okay," he said with a nod. He wiped his hands on a napkin, took a quick drink of his soda, and stood. "Let's go."

"Go?"

"To the falls." He nodded toward the front door, where Fryer Tuck's bell chimed. A young couple entered, two kids from the high school, one whose parents I knew well. The girl's parents never would have let her out this late on a date. But they snuggled close and looked innocently happy, and I wasn't a rule-enforcer.

"Are we going?" Gideon asked. "Before it gets dark."

He trusted me. He listened. And he wanted to follow up on my suggestion.

Partners.

I stood and marched past him toward the door, then doubled back to grab the rest of my chicken wrap. He eyed me with amusement, and I shrugged.

"It's a long hike," I said. "You might want to fuel up."

Dirt kicked up, puffing around our feet and catching the glow of the sunset. Faint illumination streamed in through the trees that lined the trail. I'd walked it many times and didn't need much light to guide me, but Gideon stumbled along behind. His tight uniform pants and long-sleeved shirt didn't bode well for climbing the steep hill.

"You weren't kidding about this climb," he said, huffing and puffing like he was ready to blow the entire mountain down. He stopped and leaned his hands on his knees.

"I thought cops were in shape," I said with a teasing smile. He'd been so arrogant before, but that all vanished here.

"Round is a shape," he said.

"Right," I said. As if he was round at all. Did he forget I'd seen his half-naked body the first time we'd met? "Because that perfectly describes you."

"Well, I get the feeling you're not a fan of squares."

Was that a joke I heard? No, not from Gideon-the-arrogant-cop. But maybe he'd become Gideon, my partner in secret crime? He'd probably arrest me right here and handcuff me to the tree if he knew I even dared to think he'd be an accomplice to criminal activity.

"Does what I'm a fan of matter to you?" I asked. I turned back around and didn't wait for him to catch his breath. He'd survive. Though, I forgot to mention we'd need to do a bit of swimming to make it to Grayson Baird's home. He'd carved the cave as a gift, a new house for his faery bride—behind the falls.

"You're right. As a fan of the fries, I never should have trusted your judgment on those." He laughed. I half-smiled.

"Hey, you enjoyed them," I said. I glanced back to see he'd straightened and ran his hand through his hair. The haze of evening glow highlighted the veins in his arm and the curve of his muscle.

"I'd be lying if I said I didn't," he said.

I turned back around and continued up the path, following the jagged trail toward the falls. The steep climb would plateau soon, and we'd be above the tree line and able to see the view of the town in the distance. I loved the glittering lights from homes and the deafening crash of the falls. The only sound that carried up here was the drums and cheers from Folklore Fall's high school football games. But it wasn't Friday, and the only sound until we reached the falls was Gideon's breath and the faint rustle of trees.

The closer we became, the more excited I was to share this investigation with him. As a professional, Gideon could track the dagger down twice as fast as me. Maybe he'd even end up arresting the Jensens for stealing it.

"We should turn around," he said, putting his hand to his forehead and looking out over the valley. "It will get dark before we get back."

"We're close," I said. We couldn't turn back. I'd finally convinced him to look into the artifact, which was a gigantic leap considering many didn't even believe it existed. I wouldn't give up this opportunity. "If you hurry, we can make it."

Gideon checked the watch on his wrist, then twisted his brows into a skeptical look.

"It's worth it," I said. "Trust me." As soon as I said it, I recalled what he'd said. I could listen carefully, too. Gideon had admitted he didn't trust easily, and yet, he let me take him all the way out in the middle of nowhere on my hunch—lie—that the dagger's thief was also the vacationer's thief. That was if he continued to follow.

The footsteps that followed confirmed his trust in me.

A twinge of pain built in my chest, but it wasn't from a struggle to breathe or acid reflux. I'd eaten the chicken wrap, not the greasy fries —from Gideon's good influence. So, if it wasn't heartburn…

Once we reached the falls, I broke the bad news. We stood in a crowd of rocks closest to the trail. The spot was only a quarter way up the falls' height and made for a perfect jumping point. Another step forward, and we could leap off the rock and land in the pool below.

Gideon only laughed. "You want me to swim in my uniform past the waterfall to see a rock?"

"I thought we could find a pattern from the vandalism there with the break-ins." *Lie.* Of course, I knew a pattern didn't exist between the two, but if he found a new clue, maybe he'd go deeper into the dagger investigation. Besides, I'd take any excuse to visit the falls and go for a night swim.

I slipped my shoes off and bent to yank my socks from my feet.

"What're you doing?" he asked, eyebrows angled.

"Jumping in," I said.

Gideon shook his head. "No. No way. Relaxed is one thing, but this is too much for me."

"Swimming is too much?"

"This is a state park. That means staying here after dark and without a permit to swim is against the law."

I shrugged, turned, and stepped to the edge of the rock. "So is taking the dagger."

"Two wrongs—"

"I don't care." I bent my legs ready to slip over the edge of the rock. Instead of cool water and the rush of the fall, I felt a warm hand grip around my wrist.

"Excuse me," I said, yanking my arm from him. "You're not stopping me."

"This is illegal—"

"It's important." I pointed toward the falls where Baird's dagger had once been stored. "This is our town's history."

When I turned, the process repeated. Except this time, it wasn't a warm hand that slapped around my wrist. The clink of metal chimed like a bell, barely loud enough to register over the crash of the falls.

The cold metal burned against the flesh on my wrist, and I snapped my head back to see Gideon had secured one half of a set of handcuffs on me.

"I can't watch you do something against the law," he said.

My jaw dropped, but I refused to let shock paralyze me. I used the connection between us to pull him toward me. The reaction startled him, and my sleight of hand combined to make the perfect storm. I stood in the eye of it while he was trapped in the turmoil. In one smooth move, I'd grabbed hold of the handcuffs and slapped them on his wrist.

Gideon gasped, and the heat of his breath warmed my face as he exhaled and blinked at me in surprise. I took a step back, feeling the edge of the rock with my bare heel. Once he got wet, he'd give in.

I think.

Understanding dawned on Gideon's face. His dark eyes glittered with shock.

"No—"

I offered an apologetic smile before jumping. Gravity and the element of surprise aided in my slight figure pulling his bulky body down with me. The brief fall combined with the chilly water sent a ripple of adrenaline through my veins.

We burst through the surface, gasping for breath. Gideon reached up to wipe his wet, overgrown hair from his face. It tugged me toward him, and he blinked his eyes open as my body pressed against him. The reminder of our situation left him flushed.

Droplets balanced precariously on his eyelashes until he blinked them away. I dipped the back of my head into the water, then used my free arm to pull the hair from my neck and face. When I came up again, he hadn't moved. Distance didn't exist between us.

He grunted, and a rush of air came from his nose. "You broke the law."

"It's for a good cause," I said, searching his eyes. *Trust me. Just long enough to solve this.* We'd find the dagger and save the town.

And then he'll leave.

I chewed on my lip, and his eyes flickered to my mouth.

"This is wrong."

His gaze didn't leave my lips when he said it. My breaths came in shallow bursts as I waded to stay above the surface.

"We're in the water now. Just let me show you," I said.

Gideon swallowed and glanced toward the falls. The spray of water dotted our faces with droplets, and the never-ending mist kept my hair glued to my neck.

"This isn't part of my investigation," he said.

"Then, why did you follow me up here?"

He broke our gaze and looked away from me again, pursing his lips.

"Please," I said.

Instead of responding, he pulled me closer to him. His eyes met mine, and I felt his hand bump mine beneath the water. The water darkened his brown hair to black and the light of the moon caught the cut of his cheekbone that I noticed was only visible with the hint of a smile.

Was he enjoying this? And which part? Denying me the one thing I wanted or something else?

Our gaze didn't break until the clamp of the handcuffs was released. He'd unlocked us.

"Okay," he said.

I furrowed my brows, and the scar on his mouth disappeared into the smile line with his smirk.

"You helped me," he said. "So, I'll help you."

"Really?"

"I don't like to be in debt to anyone."

Right. Did the debt have anything to do with the way his gaze kept slipping beneath my neck? My gray shirt was plastered against my skin, showing every curve and angle of my torso.

Whether or not it was the truth, I'd take it. I nodded toward the falls, extended my arms, and swam forward. By the time we made it around the crashing water, we were both heaving.

The cave welcomed us with cover from the breeze that picked up over the mountain at night. We climbed onto the slanted rocks and lay side-by-side, catching our breaths.

Moonlight illuminated the backside of the falls with a bluish glow, and the eternal ripples in the water sent dancing lights around the cave. The effect took me back to diamonds and proposals and engagement rings.

"It's stunning," Gideon said, breaking the silence between us. He stood, and I hurried to my feet, eager to share the legend that I loved so much. Some little girls dream about their wedding day. I dreamed about Baird's and Ellery's.

"Isn't it?" I echoed. "This is where Grayson married her." Excited, I grabbed Gideon's shoulders with both of my hands and positioned him on the edge of the rock, nearest the backside of the falls.

"This is where he stood," I said, then pointed to the outcropping above and behind his head. "And the story says Oberon and Titiana themselves came with their blessing. They watched from there." I stepped closer to him. "And this is where I believe Ellery was when they said their vows."

Gideon grabbed my arms, which forced my attention on him. My chest heaved from the hurried explanation, adrenaline, and excitement of being back in Baird's cave. I expected him to snap at me for losing focus and demand I show him the rock with the cut of the dagger. But his eyes were soft as he held my gaze.

"Slow down," he said. "I can't even understand what you're saying."

"This is my favorite place in the world," I said. I sighed at the sight I'd seen a hundred and one times. The backside of the falls, coupled with the smooth rock and moonlight, came as close to how I imagined the faery realm might look.

"I can tell."

I snuck a glance at him. Gideon wasn't looking at the falls.

"Why is this so important to you?" he asked. Others had questioned me about this before, but his tone didn't come with confusion or mocking, just curiosity.

I shook my head and broke our gaze. The falls captured my attention, but I was keenly aware of his eyes on me. I didn't open up to strangers, definitely not outsiders. But Gideon didn't sound malicious, and he looked at me like he listened to my every word intending to understand. It didn't matter how much I shared. He'd be gone within a week anyway. At least, that was his original deadline to find the thief.

"My parents split when I was in middle school," I said. "I was just old enough to understand romantic love, but young enough to believe in fairy tales. I went on a field trip to the falls with my class and saw the dagger in the rock and… I don't know." I shrugged and frowned. "I wanted to believe someone could love another person enough to spend decades carving into a mountain for them. Now that I'm an adult, I respect the history and want to make sure the artifact finds its way to a museum where more people can learn about Folklore Falls and hear the legend."

Gideon nodded. "That makes sense."

"Does it?" I laughed. "Not many people agree with you on that." I turned to face him, finally tearing my eyes from the crashing water.

"Not many people can stand to be around me for more than a day since…" his voice trailed, and he glanced at his feet. The handcuffs hung limp in his grip and droplets trailed down his neck. "Thank you for sharing this with me. And for putting up with me. I know I'm not the easiest person to deal with."

I wanted him to look at me again, so I could see the reflection of the falls in his eyes and how it lit him up from the inside out. As if he'd read my mind, Gideon's eyes flicked up, and he lifted his chin.

His mouth was open in a small pout. Air left my lungs as he leaned into me. The tension of what would come buzzed inside my chest, and I knew the moment before our kiss would be my favorite because we'd yet to close our eyes. I enjoyed the view but wanted more, too.

My eyelids dropped as our lips met. He tasted crisp with an earthy undertone like the fresh water of the falls. I didn't want it to end. I pressed myself into him, our wet clothes sticking to one another. Warmth filled me and my hand found his jawline while his fingers threaded through the hair at the back of my neck. The handcuffs hung from his thumb and clinked at my ear—completely forgotten by him. His other palm slipped down my back and gently pressed against my lower back, bringing me closer to him. Everything came to an end all at once and I was left breathless.

Gideon stepped back, ending it abruptly and with a gasp for air.

"I don't know what I was thinking," he said, shaking his head. "I'm sorry."

I'm not. Not yet anyway. But he'd leave Folklore Falls soon, and I'd regret it, eventually.

"That was inappropriate," he said. "I don't want to risk your status at the station."

My "job." *Right.* I nodded, then sucked in a sharp breath and licked my lips.

"The dagger," I said, pointing behind him. "Here's the rock."

I pushed past him and knelt beside the rock that had been split open with a pickax. It scarred the smooth stone with the shape of the jagged blade. My fingers found the divots and traced the place of the dagger's absence.

I didn't want to look at Gideon for fear of seeing regret in his eyes, yet it took everything I had not to grab his face and taste him again.

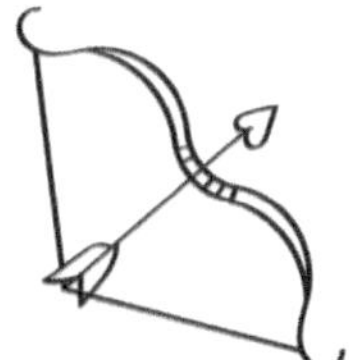

Twelve

Powdered sugar fell like a light dusting of snow over the waffles' ridges. I topped the breakfast with plump, red strawberries from the patch behind the B and B. My mouth watered at the sight of the fresh meal as I carried it to two lovely gentlemen on their ten-year anniversary trip. I'd skipped breakfast in favor of an early morning arrival.

The couple by the window beamed at me. Their bright T-shirts read *Sorry, he's taken* in matching colors.

"Fuel up for that hike," I said as I placed the plates in front of them. "Our storms are dangerous around here so you really need to make it back before the clouds roll in."

Mr. Pin nodded and his husband mirrored his agreement. "Will do, Miss Loxley. We take your advice seriously. We just love the romance in the local legend and wanted to see the falls for ourselves."

My heart warmed at the mention of our town's beloved history. If I could take a day off, I'd give these two a free tour and guide their hike. But I needed every spare second to locate the dagger in the least suspicious ways possible. With Gideon around, I'd resorted to trading stories like an info broker and reserving break-ins only when absolutely necessary.

"Legend says that if you catch the sunrise reflecting on the falls, you can see into the faery realm where Grayson Baird and Ellery are still alive." I smiled.

"It sounds silly but our marriage has me convinced magic exists," Mr. Pin said with a wink at his husband. "Maybe tomorrow we'll make it out before sunrise. If you're not busy with a meeting."

Mr. Pin's husband shook his head. "Are you kidding me? I canceled everything for this trip. I'm here to give you my undivided attention. No work."

Mr. Pin reached for his husband's hand across the table and gave it a squeeze. Tears lined his eyelids. The look shared between the couple struck my heart and caused it to skip a beat. I cleared my throat and took a breath to gather myself. I'd successfully shoved all emotion about the kiss down into an imaginary safe that even I couldn't crack. But the love between this couple did the trick.

My stomach twisted, and I no longer regretted skipping breakfast. The moment our lips had separated, guilt settled in and I didn't want to lie to Gideon any longer.

"I think we're all good here." Mr. Pin's voice was kind but the suggestion rang clear. He wanted a romantic breakfast alone with his husband and that didn't include the presence of a zoned-out server who couldn't get her mind off a particular police officer.

I swallowed and nodded, offering them a smile before darting back into the kitchen. I sucked in a cleansing breath and rubbed my hands over my forehead to push back a flyway strand of hair.

I took out the borrowed ring from the pawnshop and slipped it back on my finger. It was once a placeholder so creepy men wouldn't hit on me at the casino and the rich women would think I fit in. Now it was only a reminder of the life of lies I led. The lies that would hurt the only man I'd ever met who cared about helping others as much as I did. Plus, nobody listened to me as carefully as he did.

The ring didn't look right, especially not on the finger reserved for the symbol of love and commitment. The only thing I was committed to right now was putting space between us so I didn't want to kiss

Gideon again. Out of sight, out of mind. I tugged the ring off and shoved it into my pants pocket.

I busied myself with a dishrag and the pile of dirty plates stacked by the sink. Warm water washed over my knuckles. The bubbles that gathered in the sink matched the foam at the base of the falls. The mindless chore kept my hands moving but didn't distract my memory. Gideon would tease me about my work-life balance if he knew I'd arrived three hours before my shift at the B and B, and I'd shoot right back at him with a clean-chill balance problem. I'd learned Gideon couldn't relax if a room was messy, including his shoes left on the floor.

The first person I wanted to call after hearing Mr. Pin's declaration about magic was Gideon. For a guy obsessed with work, the cop enjoyed hearing the folklore stories so much I thought he believed them. If things were different—if Gideon was just a friend, and I wasn't a thief, we could join Mr. Pin and his husband on a sunrise hike. We could try to catch a glimpse of the supposed faery realm and—real or not—he'd enjoy it, because Gideon liked stories.

The kitchen door slammed into the wall as it swung open. Mama heaved and gestured wildly with her hands.

"A pipe burst. In one of the guest's rooms. 221. I need you to get everything out of the room before water damage sets in." She furiously tapped the screen on her phone. "I'm calling Peter."

I slapped the dishrag over the edge of the sink and wiped my hands on the apron as I pushed through the door. I took the stairs two at a time. The local handyman would do his best, but Peter worked slowly. It'd be a miracle if we could save the room's original flooring. I refused to let the furniture go with it.

The number my mom said dawned on me when I made it to the top of the stairs. A shirtless Gideon stood in the doorway wearing a tight pair of pajama pants. His glistening skin signaled that the pipe had likely burst while he was in the shower. Water still dripped from his disheveled hair.

"I have to move the furniture," I said, dodging past him into the room. I glanced into the bathroom. Water gushed from the shower, slowly seeping the floor in the next room. The carpet squished under my feet as I stepped too close to the bathroom.

"No, you need to shut off your main water valve." Gideon refused to move from the doorway, stubborn and entirely too attractive for me to look at right now.

I picked up the nightstand and nodded for him to move out of the way.

"We can't." I struggled to get around him but Gideon took the nightstand out of my arms instead.

"What do you mean you can't?" He followed me back into the room and grabbed the opposite end of the dresser, shooting me a concerned look while subconsciously following my points and nods. Together, we lifted the dresser and he shuffled backward while I grunted which direction to angle himself to fit through the doorway.

We dropped the dresser in the hall and went for the bed next.

"We're in the middle of remodeling the basement to make it into a game-hall room. There's a new wall partially blocking where the valve is. We've been meaning to finish it for weeks now but there's never enough time in the day and our handyman is a slow worker. He knows how to get to it without wrecking the new wall."

"A game hall?" he grunted while he yanked at the other end of the bed, and we scooted it toward the door. We moved in tandem, flipping the mattress on its side so we could slide it through. Pillows and sheets lay in a pile on the opposite side of the room.

"We have to compete with Jensen Resort somehow," I said with a gasp for air.

We returned to the room, bumping arms as we both went for the doorway at the same time. Gideon stepped back and let me enter. We heaved the bed frame on its side and shoved it toward the hall.

"Pivot," I said.

"I am." He bumped into the wall.

"You're not pivoting!"

Water reached the center of the room now. With every step I took, the carpet squelched beneath my feet.

"We need to get to that valve," he said.

"Not before we save this furniture. They're antiques from the original hotel."

"I know." He nodded as we eased the frame through the door without scratching the walls. "It's why I chose this place to stay. I like old things."

"Good," I said, waving for him to follow me. "Then you can help me figure out how to get to the valve. Because it's in the oldest part of the building."

"Let me grab a shirt."

"No time," I tossed the words over my shoulder. *Not a lie.* I'd have preferred him to get dressed so I could keep my mind—and my eyes—off him.

Gideon followed me to the basement where the new wall pinched the water valve between the beams of the old wall.

"We can't get to that." He sighed.

"I told you."

"You told me." He nodded.

"We're going to have to break it." I made for the stairs.

"Where are you going?"

"There's an ax in the shed outside."

"We can—"

But I was already up the stairs and pushing through the door. When I returned minutes later, Gideon was scratching his head and pacing beside the wall.

"There has to be a way to do this without ruining what you've built."

"Nope." I hoisted the fire ax in the air. Before I could bury the sharp end into the wall, Gideon shouted.

"Wait!" He shot out his hand. "Just let me think a moment longer."

"We don't have a moment. I'm cutting it down."

Gideon groaned. "This is my fault. Let me figure it out."

I paused, dropping my arm and letting the ax hang limply by my side. "It's not your fault."

His dark eyes pierced through me and flickered over my lips then back to meet my gaze. "It is. I messed up."

"It's just a pipe—"

"I won't let it wreck your job! And our—" he stopped.

My mouth hung open. This wasn't about a burst pipe. *Our what?* Friendship? Partnership? No, it could be something more and we both knew it. We could have fried ourselves with the electricity that came with that kiss so close to the falls.

"Here to save the day!" Peter's voice rang from the top of the stairs. The short man bounded down the steps and pushed between Gideon and me. He pulled a thick, bendable wire from his bag and used it to reach between the walls. I glanced at the handyman but Gideon's gaze remained. Peter snaked the wire to hook around the valve and then yanked. It was really that simple but neither Gideon nor I were in the right headspace to think clearly.

We were in a gray area now—coworkers who kissed. And clueless as to how to navigate it.

Silence hung between us as we climb the stairs to the main floor and then to the second story. *My job. My* job. I turned his words over and over in my head. That one stuck out the most, a sore reminder of my lie. A lie that Gideon didn't deserve to be told.

Mama set Gideon up in a new room but he insisted on helping us move the furniture to the basement before finishing his shower. Mama and Peter's presence kept us from discussing anything beyond the weather and water damage. And it was just as well—I needed to put space between us.

I'd wrecked my relationship with my ex with deceit and sneaky behavior—I didn't dare risk the friendship Gideon and I had developed. We'd stay at a distance, only touching on small talk and discussing the investigation. Or not even that.

The more time we spent together, the harder it would be to keep up the facade without guilt melting me like the Wicked Witch of the West.

"Loxley," Gideon said as we started to part ways at the top of the basement. I headed for the desk in the lobby. He followed after closing the door to block the eyesore of furniture storage that the basement had become. So much for competing with Jensen Resort.

I shuffled the pamphlets on the desk around, though they were already straightened and in place.

"Hmm?"

"Dinner tonight?" he asked. "No investigation talk. Work-life balance practice, right? Just friends sharing a meal." The small smile made his scar disappear.

Yes. I'd love that. Dinner and a walk through the forest. I already knew how deliciously the moonlight highlighted the muscles in his arms. Plus, how the night sky brought out the dark shade of his eyes.

Fox in a henhouse.

"I'll call you," I said. *Lie.* Because I couldn't lie to him anymore.

Gideon's face brightened, the seriousness of it melting away. "Split a plate of fries?"

I nodded, but I was already planning how I'd move forward with my own investigation. I needed to get my mind off his mouth, his quirks, and his relentless kindness that had shattered my original expectations of him.

Gideon climbed the stairs, pausing to let an elderly couple pass him. He glanced at me, but I looked away.

Ditching the investigation meant I'd need to return to late-night appearances at the casino in Jensen Resort to gather information. Rumors and gossip threaded together would paint a clearer picture of who might have taken the dagger. I couldn't cross off the Tamsens or Evanses just yet. Since I wanted to be absolutely sure before risking a break-in at the Jensens, I needed more info.

But my mind easily wandered from the dagger and to how quickly Gideon jumped in to help me with the furniture. The cop wasn't supposed to fit in here—or with me.

Somehow, he did.

Thirteen

G rits, guests, and Grayson Baird's dagger dominated my weekdays. For the next week, I became less the cunning fox and more the chicken running around with her head cut off. I'd balanced thieving and running the Sherwood's Bed and Breakfast by sacrificing sleep and a bit of sanity. With the addition of the community service I owed Folklore Falls' PD, I'd collapse any moment. And when I found a minute to sleep, the cop and our kiss kept appearing in my dreams. I'd given myself a deadline—one more week to help with the investigation, then I was out, I'd leave Gideon in peace.

I wiped my forehead with a damp dishrag and flopped into an empty seat in the dining room. Only four weeks ago, the future Mrs. Culp had sat at this table where her dashing douchebag had proposed marriage on bended knee. The only proposal I'd received was a stakeout.

Gideon wanted to watch the homes I'd targeted most often with a full night's undercover watch, and I'd yet to figure out a solid plan to twist this toward the dagger and away from the thefts. We'd only found wood splintered from the handle of the pickax at the falls. It wasn't enough to entice Gideon to derail his entire investigation. Not yet.

I leaned back against the bay window and allowed myself to catch my breath after the morning rush. Dishes clanked from the kitchen where Mama cleaned up. Grandpa Owl's voice drifted from the entry when the front doorbell jingled.

While Gideon spent the week taking statements and watching hours of security camera videos, I had to work—my real job. Mama needed my help, but not every moment. The second Gideon noticed I had downtime, he'd call me over to this table where he sat with his laptop to tap in with my 'keen eye,' as he'd called it.

The stakeout would take place later in the week, which meant I had only a few days left to convince him to watch the Jensens' house rather than the Halls'. But to do that, I'd need to skip tonight's sleep and hit the house nearest the Jensens', giving the cop reason to believe the thief might case the area. I wasn't convinced it was the best plan, and I really needed the sleep, but it'd have to do.

I pulled out my phone, shot a quick text to Bella to see if she was available to be on lookout, then scooted to the edge of the seat. I needed a full minute to prepare myself to stand and resume the day's duties after the past few days. After a long yawn, I dropped my face into my palms and rubbed my eyes.

"Are you okay?"

I looked up to see Gideon towering over me. His dark waves hung in his face. The tightly fitted T-shirt and pressed jeans gave him a relaxed look that I'd never seen on his stiff body before. From this angle, his scar looked deeper and more jagged, like glass had cut through the edge of his lips.

Gideon furrowed his brows, and I blinked, realizing I'd been staring at his mouth.

"Are you okay?" he repeated. "You look beat." He took a seat across from me, where Mr. Culp had prepared his marriage proposal.

"Just what every woman wants to hear," I said, as I pinched the claw at the back of my head and let my hair fall. "I'm worried about my friends. You've met Sara and Diana and Billy now. He can't afford his chemo. Sara was this close," I pinched my fingers together, "to finishing law school before Jensen Resort put her tours of the falls out of business."

Gideon's eyebrow ticked, and his gaze raked over me.

"I just wanted to make sure you weren't sick," he said. "I'm sorry to hear about your friends."

Gee, thanks. I went from beat to sick in his eyes quicker than I'd snagged Mr. Culp's wallet out of his back pocket.

"Oscar the Grouch strikes again," I said. I ran my fingers through my hair to unknot the tangles before twirling it into a messy bun on the top of my head again.

Without looking, Gideon opened his laptop. He kept his gaze on me, eyes softening.

"It wasn't criticism," he said. The keyboard clicked in rhythmic droning as he booted up the program he'd been using to view the security videos.

I could only see through the reflection on his Blue-light glasses. He'd put them on whenever he watched the videos, which happened every morning this week. Except today, he was earlier than usual.

"It's practicality," he said. "I don't have time to risk catching a cold, so I asked. Besides, taking care of people you love is exhausting, and that's nothing to be ashamed of." Gideon nodded toward the kitchen where Mama washed the dishes, and he'd picked up on the routine after several days of using the dining room as his office. He adjusted his glasses after they knocked loose and tilted sideways from the nod. The thick frames enhanced his dark eyes.

"Hmm," I said with a curt nod. He wouldn't charm me with the stupid, sexy glasses.

"It's like, uh, an artifact in a museum. Weary, but admirable."

"What?" I didn't have the mental capacity for Gideon's weird way of wording things, and I had loads of blankets and sheets to wash before the weekend rush of guests. I shook my head and started to stand.

"I'd tell my fiancée the same thing when she looked pale. But she always knew, pale and sickly or not, she captivated me."

I paused midway to standing. The position reminded me of crouching over a toilet, so I straightened and coughed to clear my throat.

"Your fiancée?" My heart skipped a beat. Did I kiss a taken man? I refrained from gasping at the sudden pain the thought sent through my chest.

Gideon glanced over his glasses like an old man, and it suddenly reminded me of how awkwardly he behaved. He spoke bluntly, yet remained mysterious. He accused everybody and everything that had breath and two legs of criminal activity, but he couldn't see the thief standing right in front of him. The man was an enigma, and now he threw a fiancée into the mix.

"Not like that," he said, shaking his head. "Not now, I mean. It's been so long, I forgot she'd struggled to accept compliments. Like you."

"Like me what?" I asked, as I sat again. *Color me intrigued.* Green. That represented curiosity, right?

"You didn't take the compliment."

I shook my head. It was like Gideon carried his own conversation with me, yet I wasn't part of it. No sense.

"Never mind," he said. "I wanted to ask you to look at this video. It shows the side of the Fords' house, but something looks unusual to me."

"I'm really busy," I said, though I made no move to get up again. The dining room was quaint and homey, but not particularly comfortable. Still, I could have fallen asleep with the sun streaming in through the windows and the noise from the dishes gone. But a nap risked another dream where Gideon wore nothing but a towel and asked me if I'd use my observational skills on his body. My subconscious just went from mildly annoying to wildly inappropriate now too fast.

Fox in a henhouse. I palmed my eye and rubbed the exhaustion away.

"Copy," he said with a sad smile. That word had annoyed me before in its aggressive way to shut down a conversation, but the soft line of his mouth caused me to pause. Gideon took a deep breath and glanced from his computer to the window.

"Is something wrong?" I asked. Why? I didn't know. It wasn't my business to worry about the feelings of the cop hunting me.

Gideon blinked and licked his lips. "No. Eager to get this solved and get home."

"I bet your fiancée misses you."

He shook his head. "She's gone. Part of my past." *Did I mistake his sadness as homesickness when it was really a broken heart? Not my business.* "Anyway," he said, "if you get a moment, I'd appreciate your observational skills."

"What?" I snapped my head up from the sudden interest I'd taken in the strings of my apron.

"Are you awake, Loxley?" he asked. He removed his glasses and furrowed his brow.

I sighed, blowing the escaped strands of hair from my face. "Unfortunately." I stood and circled the table. "Okay, show me."

Gideon clicked the play button, let it roll for a moment, then slammed the Pause. He pointed to the screen where a thin object jutted from a window. I knew exactly what it was before he spoke. My throat tightened and heart raced.

"Does that look like an arrow to you?"

"No." *Lie.*

"Look closer, you're better than this," he said, jabbing the screen that showed the side of the Fords' house.

I blinked and leaned over him. His scent of sandalwood and mint matched the moment we'd first met.

"Okay, it's an arrow stuck in the window. So?" I asked, as if I didn't know the truth. I'd sent that arrow to check if the window was wedged open as it had appeared from the ground. I wasn't about to climb the trellis to find a locked window. But I never knew a camera surveyed their house from this angle.

"Do you know anyone who is adept with a bow and arrow?"

I swallowed hard and silently cursed myself for the slipup at Fryer Tuck's. Why did I tell Gideon about my talent with archery? Why did I tell him anything about me at all? He'd be leaving soon.

I gnawed on my lip and willed my racing heart to slow. Words had rescued me plenty of times before. A smooth tongue was a pickpocket's smoke and mirrors. I'd compliment a woman's handbag while slipping the watch from her wrist. Where could I direct Gideon's attention?

"From what Sheriff Max has told me, you're at the archery range a lot," he said.

I closed my eyes and grit my teeth. Sheriff Max needed to keep his big mouth shut. At the click of a button, I opened my eyes.

Gideon had resumed the video. I knew what came next.

That night, I'd worn a black zip-up sweater rather than my green hoodie. Thank goodness Grandpa Owl had insisted on repairing the frayed seam around the front pocket. My shadowed body appeared on the screen, and I scaled the side of the wall.

The lack of light, my dark clothes, and the hood covering my head and face obscured any personal details. Still, my stomach knotted in a hundred twists, turning and smashing the waffles I'd had for breakfast.

"Does this person look familiar?" Gideon asked.

"Yes," I said. *Definitely the truth.* "I bet it's Brett Jensen." Not a bet I'd ever take. But I'd just found my plan to direct Gideon toward the hunt for the dagger.

"Interesting," Gideon said. "I'll look into it." He glanced up at me, and the sword scar was missing. His smile and the beginnings of a beard concealed the jagged line. "Thank you. I'll let you get back to work, but if you're free for dinner, it's on me."

My heart skipped a beat, but I couldn't tell if it was caused by my risky lie and the fact I'd have to back it up if I went to dinner with him. Or that he believed me. And so easily. Did he suspect me but look the other way? If so… why?

Another sharp pain flickered in my chest like a bolt of lightning.

Gideon either cared about me or he trusted me, and the latter didn't sit right with me.

Fourteen

GIDEON

I paced the open space in my suite. Sherwood Bed and Breakfast had catered to my every need since I'd arrived. The water was warm, the food fresh, and the owners kind. But I'd never survive on desk duty and yet I found myself wanting to stay in Folklore Falls.

The mattress sank under my weight as I sat on the edge of the bed and dropped my head into my hands. I wasn't comfortable here anymore. Conversations with Loxley felt different lately. We weren't at ease with friendly jokes or arguing over the case anymore—just tense.

"Why?" I groaned and balled my hands into fists. Why did I kiss her?

This wasn't the first time I'd let a woman derail my focus. Except with Loxley, I felt alive. It was a stark contrast to the pain of losing Marian, and the rage and fear that followed. Nothing could let me slip again. I'd fallen so far down the ranks I'd worked for years to climb.

My badge sat on the bedside table, balancing precariously on the edge. Fitting, as I was about to fall myself. I'd plummet through the ranks if I didn't solve this simple, small-town theft.

I smashed my fist against the mattress, which jostled the bed and bedside table, knocking the badge to the floor. It fell front side down.

"Idiot," I muttered to nobody but myself. I wanted to hate myself for risking my job. Right now, Loxley was a coworker, and I'd let her convince me to break the law, then I'd…

I wanted to hate her too for pulling me in, for obsessing over a silly legend, and for captivating me with it, too.

"Why did I kiss her?" I repeated, whispering into the silence of my empty room. The sun had set hours ago, and Loxley never responded to my invitation for dinner. She didn't answer her phone when I called, and the text I sent her remained in a delivered status.

I bent to pick up my badge and chucked it toward the bag by the front door. It knocked against the pocket watch and tumbled onto the floor past the bag.

From the moment we'd met, she intrigued me. She was reckless, unexplainable, and I admired her skills with investigating. Loxley thought outside of the box and yet noticed everything. I didn't think it was possible to be both reckless and intelligent.

My phone buzzed, and I shoved my hand into my pants pocket. I hurried to answer, hoping to hear her voice and praying it wasn't my sergeant from back in the city.

"Officer Notting," a deep voice said. It was neither the woman I'd hoped for, nor the woman who'd officially demote me if I didn't solve this case within the week. Sheriff Max coughed and cleared his throat. "I'm calling to inform you of a slight change in plans."

"Okay," I said. I walked to the bag by the door, but instead of picking up my badge, I took my shoes from where they hung by the laces on the key hooks. Once at the edge of the bed again, I bent forward and pulled the shoes on my feet.

"Miss Cameron will not be joining you on the investigation any longer," Sheriff Max said.

"She—" I swallowed and straightened. I'd destroyed both our professional relationship and the friendship we'd formed with reckless emotion. It was definitely me I hated. So, why couldn't I stop thinking about how soft her lips were or the sweet taste of her mouth? I gripped the phone tighter in my fist. "What happened?"

"Oh." He sighed and took forever to answer, speaking in the slow way only people from tiny towns like Folklore Falls had the patience for. "She offered to do some extra work for her time by painting the lines on the highway."

"Her time?"

Sheriff Max fell silent. He grumbled something unintelligible and took another loud breath.

"What's it called?" he asked. I heard the snap of his fingers. "Overtime. At the station. You know, working extra hours."

"I know what overtime is," I said. "I didn't—I thought we worked well together."

"Loxley likes to work alone," Sheriff Max said. He could have said the same about me, if anybody here knew me. Only *she* did. Though, I enjoyed the company of her grandfather and some of the other patrons at Sherwood Bed and Breakfast. "Be seeing you." With that, Sheriff Max hung up, and I was left sitting in my room with the screen blinking and fading to black at my ear.

I needed fresh air. I armed myself with a bottle of water and exited the bed-and-breakfast. The mountain across the highway tempted me, but I knew I'd never find my way without Loxley's guidance. Instead, I turned and marched into Sherwood Forest for a brisk walk to clear my head.

And wipe it free of the memory of Loxley's lips.

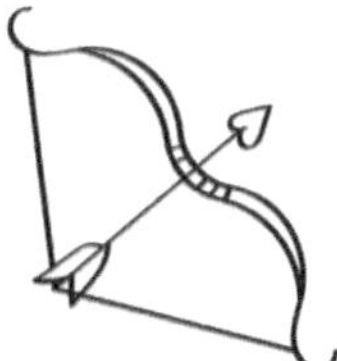

Bella and I fist-bumped as we separated. The walk to the Evanses'
house was short and sweet—meaning they lived closer to town
than most elite vacationers. The proximity made it trickier to target
their house, but the cover of nightfall, Bella's keen eye, and my preparation helped.

I pulled my phone from my pocket to set it to silent. Gideon's
number appeared on the screen with both a voicemail and a text
message. I hadn't added his name, but recognized the outside area code
as his. The voicemail played at the tap of my thumb, but I didn't finish
it before Bella whistled the go-ahead. The road was quiet, and now was
my chance.

I sent her a wave and stuffed my phone back into my pocket. I
ignored his offer for dinner, and the disappointment in the tone from
his voicemail left me wondering if he'd hoped for something more than
a business meeting. But I needed the sleep after this, and I prayed the
exhaustion would spare me from a night of dreams.

Besides, he was sorry he kissed me. He regretted the moment we'd
shared.

The Evanses' house permanently smelled of pine since they'd left
their Christmas tree to die in the front window. They had the money

to pay someone, but Mr. Evans was one of those old men who wanted to do everything himself, which also meant their security system was lacking since he didn't understood new technology. Plus, he'd never gotten around to disposing of the tree. I spotted their dog poop key cover within seconds, retrieved the key, and opened their front door.

Once inside, I realized their lack of need for the extensive cameras and security systems of the Jensens or other elite vacationers. The Evans kept nothing of value here—not monetary value anyway. Photographs covered their walls, mantel, and every tabletop. A family of dark-haired, smiling faces beamed down at me from the trail of frames along the staircase. The photos circled the largest frame that held a stunning black-and-white photograph, retouched and blown up, showing Mr. and Mrs. Evans's simple wedding.

The Robin's whistle signaled, and I peeked my head out the front door. Bella shot me a thumbs up from her lookout location by the gate. It cleared me to investigate for a few more minutes.

I poked around the large cabin and spotted a safe. After listening carefully, twisting and turning and waiting for the clicks, I almost gave up. It wasn't likely they had the dagger. But the dial clunked and released the door. I opened to find a wealth of jewelry—old-fashioned but expensive gold pocket watches and a locket with the same wedding photo inside.

I sighed, dropped the items back inside the safe, and locked it. With the extra time, I dragged the dead tree from its spot by the window. Pine needles rained down into a trail along the cabin's floor and porch.

Bella's whistle sounded again. She twisted her face in confusion and threw her hands up. "What the hell?"

I huffed and dumped the tree at the bottom of the porch. "It's a fire hazard," I shouted, then lowered my voice and mumbled to myself. "I couldn't let it burn all those photos."

Mr. and Mrs. Evans looked so happy, so in love in when they married. And from what I'd seen of them when I pickpocketed my way through the elite clique, they still did. I never targeted them, and it was a relief to know they didn't take the dagger. So, why didn't I feel relieved? Tension clung to my ribcage like trapped butterflies since Baird's cave, and a lump continued to build in the pit of my stomach.

I'd even lost my appetite for waffles and Fryer Tuck's milkshakes. Since Gideon, all I could stomach was plain chicken wraps. He'd kissed me. He *trusted* me when he shouldn't. My stomach twisted and knotted tighter. I took one last look at Mr. and Mrs. Evans locked in a timeless moment right before a kiss. The moment before *our* kiss stuck with me, and the same nerves and joy and desire flickered in my chest.

I locked the door, returned the key under the plastic dog poop, and hopped over to Bella.

"A waste of time?" she asked with raised brows. She straightened from leaning against the gatepost and folded her book shut before following me.

"Not for their insurance company," I mumbled.

"So, we're a Christmas tree disposal service now," she said. "I want my cut." She held out her palm, and I slapped it with a high five. "Lox, what's up with you?"

"Nothing." I shrugged. We hiked up the dirt road toward the town. "I'm not a terrible person. I couldn't let their house burn down."

"I know that," she said, jogging up beside me. I wasn't tall, but to Bella, I may as well have been a tree. "Nobody said you're a terrible person. We only target the cruel people. I'm talking about this pout you've had permanently tattooed on your face."

I swatted her finger away from me and shot her a sharp look. I hadn't wanted to trade my time with Gideon for painting the highway lines. It took everything I had to call Sheriff Max and ask for a negotiation about my community service. Gideon didn't deserve to be tricked. Just like with Mama and the Culps' business at the B and B, I couldn't risk the people I cared about. I'd find the dagger on my own and leave the cop in peace before he left me for the city.

"I'm just tired," I said. *Lie.*

"So, you don't want to head to Knight's for a beer?" she asked, referring to our tradition of celebration. We'd find any excuse to go to the tavern, whether it was a successful steal from a snobby vacationer or a break-in that yielded nothing, after which I'd claim we needed a drink to cool off. "I say we take that challenge with Katrina and Bones in darts. He promised to read an entire book if we win. It's an automatic sale for the shop."

Gravel crunched under our feet. Summer nights weren't warm yet, and a cool breeze left me with goosebumps along my bare arms.

"Another time," I said, smiling with my promise. "I'm going to cut through Sherwood and check in on Grandpa Owl and Mama before I crash at home for the night. Good run tonight, though. We've narrowed it down. The Jensens definitely have it."

Bella nodded and said goodbye with another fist-bump. She flipped her book open again and read by the light of the almost-full moon as we split and she took the road toward the other side of town, closer to Knight's Tavern.

Trees blocked most of the night's natural light in Sherwood Forest, but I didn't pull out my phone. I didn't want to see Gideon's name, knowing I'd give in to the temptation to call him back.

I ran my hand along the bark of a tree, smiled at the sound of an owl, and enjoyed the distraction. Thinking of Gideon sparked a strange mixture of guilt and excitement. It didn't match up and left me with a sour stomach.

If I had any energy, I'd blow this feeling off with a night at the archery range.

I itched to look at my messages, but when I stuck my hand in my pocket, a noise alerted me. Bears rarely came into Sherwood Forest since the houses and town surrounded it, but it wasn't impossible.

I froze and listened. A sigh followed the crunch of leaves, and my muscles melted. It was only a person. The shadowed figure of a bi-pedaled creature confirmed my relief as they crossed the trees several yards in front of me.

When I opened my mouth to say hello, nothing came out. The light of the person's phone illuminated their face just enough for me to see the sword-shaped scar.

My phone buzzed. I held my breath, not wanting to see him right now, and pressed my back against a tree trunk. I pulled out my phone to see he'd messaged me again.

Loxley. He started the text with an address to my name—always official and formal, as if he were Mr. Darcy himself.

I apologize for my behavior. It was unprofessional and a mistake.

I flicked the side button on my phone to change it from vibration to silent. The crunch of his footsteps came closer, but I wasn't ready to see him. I couldn't explain why I ditched him for painting highway lines because he could never know the truth and I didn't have the energy to lie.

Fox in a henhouse. I didn't have the stomach to lie. Not to him. Not right now.

His footsteps came closer. I pressed the screen to my chest to block the light in case he texted me again.

He sighed and stood close enough for me to smell the sandalwood and mint, his permanent smell. The damp soil of Sherwood threw an earthy scent into the mixture that sent me back to Baird's cave—to our kiss.

I closed my eyes and chewed on my lip. Gideon had stopped, and the only sound was his breathing and the rustle of wind through the leaves. Sherwood always mimicked the falls at night. Even in the summer, the warm breeze made the leaves dance.

A sudden and blaring song exploded through the sounds of nature. I gasped and slapped my hand over my mouth—I was practiced at sneaking, but Gideon threw me off my game.

"Officer Notting," he said, answering the call. A moment of silence followed, and I dared to check my phone but tucked it inside my shirt to keep the glow contained.

"I'll stay here if I have to," he said. "I will solve this." He sighed, and I imagined he raked his fingers through his hair as he did every time he exhaled in exasperation. Though, I had gotten used to that exasperation being directed at my sarcasm and teasing in the last week.

"Give me another chance," he said. "This weekend, a potential suspect will be back in town. I'd like the opportunity to stakeout the house."

Who? Was he referring to Brett Jensen? My stomach twisted. I'd lied about that, leading him where I wanted him.

Except, maybe it'd work. With his expertise, and my trickery, we could upend the Jensens and watch their behavior. I had little time left to slip into the scene at Jensen Resort and spread rumors, tap into the gossip and trigger a panic. If they had the dagger, and I convinced them Gideon was on their scent, it could sniff them out and force them to return the artifact back to its original location, or even better— cancel their meeting and keep it on the premises where I could find it the night of the Gala.

With the focus taken from me and the artifact sold to a museum to cover the cost of the resident's struggles, I'd be home free. I could stop stealing, and maybe, just maybe, Gideon and I could be friends.

"Thank you," he said. "I won't let you down."

I won't let you down. I echoed his promise in my head, except I couldn't guarantee I'd be able to uphold mine. This was a lot of ifs. I thrived on a challenge, and *if* I could give Gideon a reason to trust me, it would be worth it.

His footsteps faded, and the pounding in my heart picked up, excited for the potential the new plan held. Forget painting highway lines. I was back on the investigation and wouldn't miss the stakeout for anything.

Sixteen

Jensen Resort was all glam and no substance. The floors sparkled, and the ceiling peaked, but it didn't fit with Folklore Falls. It didn't suck you into the town's charm and beg you to see the falls or Baird's cave. Shiny surfaces enchanted the resort's patrons and blinded them to the true beauty of the nature and history here.

It was easy to slip among them. I'd changed into a whole other being—the cunning fox invisible until I pounced on the chickens. With brand name clothes, my hair slicked into a tight bun, expensive jewelry borrowed from Pop's, and a pinched, judgmental expression, I looked nothing like the green hoodie-wearing girl with powdered sugar in her hair and a quiver on her back.

The resort housed a small casino, so I made my way into the gambling crowd. The low-cut gown drew attention from wandering eyes while my lying diverted attention from the games. I played the innocent, and nobody could call my bluff, and even though I could lie that the gown made by Grandpa Owl was an original Marchesa design, my focus was elsewhere. I never stayed winning for too long.

I pretended to sip at the wine and joined a conversation of women over Texas Hold'em. They laughed and discussed the eyesore on

Highway Four, AKA Sherwood B and B. I coughed on the chardonnay, then forced a smile when all eyes turned on me.

"I've wondered why the Jensens don't buy out that place," I said, trading the glass for my cards in my hand.

An unnatural blonde raised her eyebrows and clucked her tongue. She leaned over the table and lowered her voice. "I heard the Jensens could go bankrupt."

A slight woman with shiny-black hair shook her head. "They went overboard on this place, but I can't say I hate it."

"So, why don't they just raise their prices?" I asked. It was the wrong question. All eyes locked on me. Injected lips pursed, and they exchanged glances with one another. I thought I could fit in, but here, I was an outsider. I only hoped it wasn't as obvious as the construction tarps and gates marking the resort.

"That's the point of the grand reopening, dear," Blondie said. She spoke in a voice one might use to explain basic concepts to a child. "If they can pull it off with the added renovations, they'll get back what they put into this place with the hiked rates. Though, it's still a mystery, even to me, why they'd host the reopening at the estate rather than the resort itself."

I nodded. "Right." I lifted the glass and gave the wine a little swirl. "I've had too much wine."

The women laughed at that, and we played another round. I wanted to slip the pearl bracelet from Blondie's wrist but averted my eyes. I was here with a plan, and it wasn't pickpocketing.

Instead, I sipped the white wine and smiled. "I suppose it makes sense why they stole the artifact then."

Blondie arched an eyebrow while the others went slack at the lips. They all stared at me, waiting for another drop of juicy gossip.

"What artifact?" Blondie tapped her long fingernails against the stem of her cocktail glass.

"Grayson Baird's dagger," I said. My voice had lost its careful edge, and I'd descended into the legend fan girl. I cleared my throat and tried again. "You know that silly legend from Folklore's history?"

They all nodded, not wanting to be the one who didn't know.

"Well, I caught wind that they took it and that cop in town is on their trail."

Blondie smirked. "I knew they couldn't stay on top forever." She played her cards and won the round again, taking the pot of chips into her arms. The women dispersed, and I expected them to spread the rumor like bees carrying pollen.

The best part was that the plants would take root right here in the Jensen's own resort. The gossip would reach them soon enough. All I had to do was hope it'd reach them by Friday.

I swirled the wine and finished the glass. After a round of poker and two losses in blackjack, I mentioned the cop four more times— winning at my game of gossip and lies.

It took less than two hours for the gossip to come back to me as a drunk woman in a red pantsuit, exactly like the one I'd taken from the resort's lost and found, stumbled over her words.

"I'd love to see Brett Jensen in handcuffs," she said, slurring the words together. "Of course, I'd want him for myself instead of in that rickety old jail." She laughed and took another gulp of a margarita that left a line of salt on her plumped lips. I joined the joke with fake laughter to hide my grimace. Who could love that prick of a man? The worst part about the Jensens was that they grew up here, attending the same elementary and high school as I did. But they had family money, and when Grandfather Jensen died, they came into more money that I could even fathom. That was when they turned their back on the town.

Before the money, Brett was a friendly boy. Currency was a curse that changed him and the rest of his family into beasts.

A man echoed the drunk woman's words about Brett Jensen in handcuffs.

"Maybe if he returns the artifact, he'll spare himself the trouble. No rickety old jail for him," I said.

The man nodded and confirmed the rumors I'd originally been following. "They've been bragging that they own this town for weeks now," he said. "I thought it was all a show with no tell, but Elaine said they have a big announcement after the reopening."

I leaned forward and almost tipped off the tall chair. The wine left my head spinning, and I regretted I didn't have a clear head. "What announcement?" Did it have to do with the meeting the housekeeper mentioned?

He didn't react, or so I thought. The slight tug at the skin on his temples told me he tried to raise his eyebrows, but a recent round of Botox had frozen his face. He glanced around and lowered his voice.

"She was high on painkillers after another reconstruction on her face when she said it, so I have no idea how outlandish this is." He paused and licked his lips, then gave me a small wink. "Usually what goes on between Doctor Brown's plastic surgery patients in recovery stays between Doctor Brown's plastic surgery patients in recovery, but I've had my eye on Brett forever, and this only solidifies that edgy side of him I've always been drawn to."

I had no idea what any of that meant other than this man's obvious crush on the youngest son of the Jensen family. The elite lived in an entirely different world than I did with reconstructed body parts, offshore bank accounts, and multiple homes.

"Apparently, Brett found the dagger from that old legend when he was a kid. He likes to joke and say it only exists in a book."

My breath caught in my throat. The memory of our fifth-grade field trip came flooding back. Brett was teasing me for wearing shoes with holes while following me around the cave. I'd found the markings on the rock Baird forged together with what I assumed as a child was faery power. The tip of the blade was jutting from the rock, and I'd cut my finger when I turned the rock over. I'd thought Brett was gone, but maybe not.

"My bet is they're going to sell it discreetly for a chunk of change, though it'll be worth a lot more than what they need to clear their bankruptcy. I'm guessing they'll open more resorts throughout the States," he said. With that, he polished off his blue cocktail, then popped the cherry from the bottom into his mouth.

"I bet you're right," I said, boosting his ego to encourage him to continue talking about it. I draped my hand on his forearm and met his gaze, ready to be honest for once. "But Brett's a beast," I said. "You can do better."

The guy half-smiled and nodded. He raised his empty glass to me and clinked it against mine, then thanked me.

I stood, satisfied my words had done their damage, and slipped out into a quiet exit. Considering I'd snuck the chips from others and lost most, I didn't care to cash in the measly few I had left.

Outside, the fresh air filled my lungs, and I wanted to strip from the gown and rid myself of the cigarette smell and too much perfume. I pulled the hoodie from my oversized bag—another treasure left in the lost and found by an inebriated woman, and switched out clothes in my car. Instead of driving straight home, I parked at the bottom of the mountain and hiked up.

The late-night swim cleared my mind and washed the stench of Jensen Resort from my hair. I was eager for the Jensens to arrive at their estate and for Friday to come.

I pulled myself onto the slanted rock and left my legs dangling in the water. The backside of the falls took my breath away as though I hadn't seen it a hundred and two times. Or was it the memory of Gideon leaning into me?

If I was honest with myself, I was eager to see him again. The plan was working perfectly. I always wanted to take down the Jensen's for what their resort did to my town, and now that I knew they had the dagger, that desire doubled. I never expected to make a friend in the process. Once I located the dagger, I'd never need to steal for the townspeople again.

Sara would get to finish her last semester in law school. Fryer Tuck could pay rent and stay open. Billy would reopen the bowling alley and get the upgrades necessary to draw the crowd from the resort. Diana might even consider opening the bakery again.

I'd stop breaking the law, and Gideon would never need to know I was the thief he hunted.

Seventeen

The next Friday, I showed up earlier than Gideon with two coffees, a notepad of my own, and in the freshly repaired pantsuit.

Sheriff Max furrowed his brows when I plopped down on the edge of his desk, waiting for the cop's arrival. Nothing would get me down now. I'd used the night to craft a plan to guide Gideon in the direction I wanted. He was the target, and I had a quiver full of arrows. Breathe, aim, release.

My release was just around the corner, both from a life of crime and the community service.

If I'd written the plan down in my notepad the way Gideon recorded clues, it'd be all-caps, bold letters, and clipped sentences.

STAKEOUT AT JENSENS. CLUES LEAD TO DAGGER. DAGGER SOLD TO MUSEUM. BUSINESSES REOPEN. *Gideon trusts me*? The last one was wishful thinking, and probably stupid, so I erased it from my thoughts. My mind obeyed, but my heart skipped a beat at the sight of him.

Gideon shoved through the police station doors with his shoulder. With one hand at his ear and his attention on the conversation over his phone, he didn't notice me in front of him. I shifted to the edge of the desk and stood.

The hum of Sheriff Max's faint, close-lipped laugh triggered me. I shot him a sharp look, then turned back and smoothed down the wrinkles that sitting had caused to the front of the red pants.

The conversation got heated, and Gideon's free hand went to the back of his neck as he paced. He crossed the length of the single cell, walking back and forth in front of it several times.

"Copy," he said with a sigh. "Yes." Gideon pulled the phone from his ear and stared at it before pressing the edge against his forehead and closing his eyes.

I smiled and extended the coffee out as an apology for ditching the dinner he'd asked me to, as well as the investigation.

"Does the offer still stand for dinner?" I asked. "From earlier this week, I mean."

Gideon didn't even look at me or notice the coffee. He turned and swung the station's door open, letting a flood of morning sunshine in.

"I thought you were off the case," he said, brows furrowed but still not meeting my gaze.

"I wanted to help you with the stakeout," I said.

"I didn't tell—"

"Sheriff Max knows everything," I interrupted him. "Hard to believe, but that's why they made him sheriff." The corner of my eye caught Sheriff Max opening his mouth, and I wanted to shove a donut in it. I snapped my head to look at him and nodded toward the cup in my hand. "Drink this. I got it for you." *Lie.*

"Fine," Gideon said, not giving the sheriff a chance to chime in. "Let's go." The tone of his voice sent me back to the day at Jensens when he'd accused the housekeeper. I'd wanted to vomit on the stupid shoes he hung up when removed.

Maybe I was right when I'd insisted Gideon had no manners. Our conversations, his weird compliments, and that he kept flipping my expectations of him had softened me. Maybe it was time to harden again. He *had* called our kiss a mistake.

I followed him. "I've had enough of Oscar the Grouch," I said, as I yanked his car door open. He huffed as he landed in the driver's seat but still didn't look at me.

"It isn't a cute joke anymore." I took the seat opposite him. "We're partners in this, and you need to treat me with respect."

Now he looked at me. Gideon clicked the seatbelt into the holder and tilted his head like he didn't understand the word. Maybe I'd have Aretha Franklin spell it out for him.

"We have a job to do," he said. "Let's do it. I respect *that*." The Civic's engine came to life. Gideon's hand landed on the back of my seat as he watched behind us while reversing. His jaw tightened, and he drove just over the speed limit.

"I thought you didn't break the law," I said. Trees zipped by faster as we picked up speed on the highway. I pointed above the steering wheel.

Gideon grunted but eased up on the gas pedal.

"Where are we going?" I knew his job was on the line, but I didn't expect this much vitriol directed at me. Did my absence offend him that deeply? Or was it the fact that he'd regretted our moment in Baird's cave?

"Someone broke into the safe at the Fords' house months ago. I traced the stolen jewelry sold from Pop's Pawnshop. If Brett took it, we'll see in him in the security videos, and I've no doubt the owner will know who he is," he said. "It's my understanding that everyone here knows the Jensen family. And if it's not him, I'll know the owner is covering for the criminal, and I'll start by arresting him."

No. Fear struck me, and I curled my hands into fists. This plan was getting away from me, and fast.

"You can't do that," I said, not knowing how to back up the statement. But the words slipped from my mouth before I could stop myself.

"I can." He furrowed his brows. "And I will. I'm here to close this case, and we need to close it now."

My heart raced, but I willed my voice to calm and considered my words before opening my mouth. "But you want to arrest the right person. Not innocent people. Do you really want to take that risk by rushing things?"

Gideon flicked his blinker on, pulling into the lane with oncoming traffic, then zipped back over to the correct side of the road. He'd passed Falstaff, who drove slowly along the highway to observe his apple trees the lazy way—from inside of his car.

"It's more of a risk to let this crook keep wrecking the town."

"Have they stolen anything recently?" I asked, trying to drive a point home. *Slow down. Please, just leave Johnny alone.* The last theft I'd pulled was the naked statue from the Halls' house, unless you counted the dead Christmas tree. The rest were mild break-ins to scout vacation homes for any signs of the dagger.

"It doesn't matter."

"It doesn't matter that the thief may have stopped breaking the law?" I tried not to scoff at his aggressiveness. *Arrest! Arrest! Arrest!*

"They already broke the law," he said. "They deserve to be put behind bars, and I'm going to be the one to do it."

Bile rose in my throat. It tempted me to roll down a window and spit it out. Maybe it'd splatter the side of his Civic and be acidic enough to destroy the beige paint. Beige—the worst color, boring, like gold but as ugly as the hearts of the snobs who flashed their gold Tag Heuer timepieces.

"What if the thief is doing something good with the money?" I asked. It was probably stupid to throw that out there, but I couldn't help myself. I'd been slipping for a while now, letting recklessness and emotions impede my cunning. It all started with the Culps' engagement ring, and it seemed that massive rock rolled down a hill faster than I could catch it. I'd let myself get to know Gideon and live in a delusion where we could be partners.

Nothing was further from the truth.

"Impossible," he said.

"Impossible? Really?" I snapped my head from watching the trees pass and back to Gideon. "Because a person can't be more than one thing?" I used his words against him. *Nobody is just any one thing.*

Gideon glanced at me with fire in his eyes.

"They're a criminal. That's all I need to know about them."

Right. I'm nothing more. Just a criminal. As much as I tried to hold on to it, the rage faded. I closed my eyes to hold back tears. I thought we'd become friends, but it'd never last, and I knew that. He was leaving, and I was, well, a thief. But I liked our partnership, and it was the stupidest thing I'd ever done—and I'd stolen an engagement ring from my bed-and-breakfast guests.

"I really thought you were better than this," I said. It slipped from my mouth, and what did it matter now? Gideon was a robot, programmed by the law and unable to process or understand human emotions.

"So did I," he said. "But now I'll be trapped in this town on desk duty forever."

And there it was. Gideon's job meant more than catching the right person. As long as he had an arrest to report back to whoever had been on the phone earlier, he was happy—if he were capable of happiness.

As soon as we parked and Gideon stepped from the car, I whipped out my phone to text Johnny.

Brett Jensen sells to you.

Johnny: *??*

Just trust me.

I tucked my phone into my back pocket and pushed through the door, cutting Gideon off. His gentlemanly behaviors only disgusted me now. They were a farce, a mask of good behavior to cover his cold, unfeeling heart, and it reminded me of the elite vacationers with their judgments hidden behind fake smiles.

Johnny greeted us with a smile of his own. He was always genuine, though confusion tweaked this one.

"He sure does," Johnny confirmed after Gideon asked about Brett. "The Jensens have popped in here once in a while. Nobody drives Highway Four without stopping at Pop's. Get it?" He smirked at the cleverness of the Pawnshop's name. For a fierce-looking dude, Johnny was just a big teddy bear nerd.

"Why is he not in any of the videos?" Gideon asked.

Johnny glanced at me but didn't let his gaze linger. Bella emerged from the back room with the curtain swishing behind her. She immediately picked up on the tension, her eyes shifting between the three of us. This was why we worked as a band of outlaws. We could communicate without words.

And we weren't the only ones who needed a team of help…

Why didn't I think of it before? Of course, Brett Jensen wouldn't pawn his own loot. Rich people had a service for everything from maids to personal shoppers. So, why not personal sellers?

Merry. Band.

I mouthed the words we called ourselves.

Brett's.

Johnny's blank stare triggered Gideon's attention. The cop flicked his head to look at me, but Bella caught on in time.

"Because Brett has never been here," she said.

"He just said—" Gideon raised his hand to point at Johnny.

"Too much ink to the brain." Bella interrupted him and laughed as she reached up and patted her palm against the side of Johnny's bald head. He yanked away from her. "Just joking, but he meant Brett's crew, not Brett himself."

"Townsfolk refer to all of Brett's family friends as Jensens," I said, joining the story. "I've told you that." *Lie.*

"Then, I need names," Gideon said. He pulled the tiny notepad from his pocket.

If only Gideon was as terrible at his job as his superiors seemed to believe, this would be a lot easier. I could lie my lips off, but the cop would figure it out, eventually.

I offered Johnny a cringing look. He winked and whipped out the record books. Fabricated names filled the lines in between real people. At least, they weren't people I'd ever heard of around Folklore Falls.

Gideon took pictures of the notes and offered a gruff thank you to both Bella and Johnny before heading for the door.

"Lox," Johnny said. "The minute he looks up those names, he'll know they're not real."

I swallowed and nodded. "I'll figure something out."

My stomach dropped as we climbed back into the car. I felt like a lost puppy, attached to someone I shouldn't be, with the sense that he didn't want me around anymore.

"What's next?" I mustered the focus to ask.

Gideon clicked his seatbelt. The movement lifted his shirt, revealing his belt that held handcuffs and a holster with his knife.

"We'll need to find evidence connecting these people to the break-ins." He shook the flimsy notepad and then dropped it on the center console.

"Evidence," I repeated, letting my voice trail as an idea formed. Excitement laced my voice, and I shifted in the seat to face him. "You never used the splintered wood we found in the cave, right? We could see if the Jensens have a tool with a missing chunk."

"I don't have a warrant," he said.

"I can get in," I said.

Gideon furrowed his brow and glanced at me.

"I'll get the tools, and we'll have actual evidence if we can connect them."

"We'd need a warrant. A cop can't just go marching onto some-body's property and rifle through their belongings."

"Good thing I'm not a cop."

At that, Gideon screeched the car across both lanes and pulled into another alcove along Falstaff's orchard. From here, I could see the tip of the mountain that peaked just beside the falls. Gideon shoved the gear stick into park and snapped his head to look at me.

"What did you say?"

Fox in a henhouse.

"I'm an assistant," I said, smooth as ever. I wouldn't let Gideon derail me. Not now. We were so close, and I'd give him a reason to trust me as I ceased stealing. "I work at the police station, but I don't have a badge or a degree in criminal justice. So, as a civilian, I can ask to borrow some tools or poke around their pool house."

"Absolutely not," he said, shaking his head. The dark waves hung in his eyes and moved with his vehement disagreement.

"What about the Grand Reopening Gala?" I grabbed for my phone and pulled up the event information. "We can go together. You'll be undercover, enjoying an event while spying for evidence on their estate. I'll find the tool they used to cut the rock."

Gideon raked his hand through his hair. "This is insane and wrong."

"Do I need to handcuff you again?" I pointed to his belt, where he stored the cuffs and his knife.

He grimaced, and it bent the sword scar. But he didn't say no, which meant he was considering it. He needed to keep his job, and I needed that dang dagger. Win-win.

"What about the other thefts?" he asked.

I shrugged. "At least you'll have reason to question Brett, and maybe you can get a confession out of him regarding the others."

It didn't feel right to pin my crimes on the Jensens, greedy jerks or not. But I doubted Brett would admit to them anyway, and Gideon would at least have solved one major crime. With the thefts ended, maybe the case would go cold.

Gideon's nostrils flared, and he gnawed on his lip. Everything about his tense shoulders, shaking head, and frown said no, but I had one more trick up my sleeve.

I swallowed and prayed to all the gods in the universes to forgive me—especially the Brothers Grimm, since I considered fairy tales and legends my religion.

I opened my eyes and locked them with Gideon's. "Trust me."

It hurt to say it, knowing I'd lied to him all this time and had thrown his job to the edge of a cliff. This time, I wouldn't jump in and take him down with me. But I couldn't forget the people of Folklore Falls, either. The deception needed to continue just a little longer.

"So, we go," he said, scrubbing at the back of his neck, then landing his palms on the steering wheel again, "like on a date to this Gala thing, but we'll be looking for evidence?"

I nodded. "Undercover." I was confident the Jensens had the dagger, and the last place I needed to look was their estate. And if the rumors hit the family in time, they'd be scrambling to shuffle the artifact off their property before tomorrow night. The stakeout, the gala, it all lined up perfectly. Nothing could go wrong.

Except Gideon's disagreement.

I waited, holding my breath, until he finally sighed and gave me a faint nod.

"I'm running out of time," he mumbled, then met my gaze. "Okay."

I smiled. "It's a date."

As soon as he looked away, my fake happiness faded, and I dropped the forced smile.

Nothing about our friendship was real, including the one and only date we'd share. This was deeper than the lies I'd told my ex-boyfriend, and it hurt so much worse.

I swallowed a lump in my throat and tried not to think about Gideon leaving after he arrested the Jensens tomorrow.

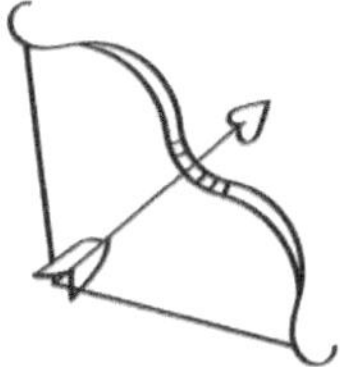

That night, I decided to be myself—not my thief persona, but the small-town, non-cop assistant in comfortable clothes, Loxley. It was as much me as I could show Gideon right now. I wanted him to know who he had a date with tomorrow—fake or not.

I pulled my old Folklore Falls archery team captain hoodie over my head, wrapped my messy hair into a plastic claw, and had grabbed a handful of snacks from Sherwood's kitchen cabinets when my shift had ended. The Cheez-Its and Teddy Grahams were for the staff, but I figured I'd worked long enough hours that week to enjoy a couple of bags.

Fish flakes spread as I dropped them into the tank and tapped the glass to say goodbye to Betty the Betta. Her red and blue scales shimmered. I longed for a quick swim myself, but I didn't have time to hike to the falls. Besides, I'd be there alone with the reminder that Gideon was a mistake.

I hurried out the door, ready for our second to last night together. Thick rain clouds had rolled in and blanketed the valley in darkness. I tugged the hood over my head and ran to the street where Gideon waited with his car. This felt like a version of a date too, with him picking me up at home.

Huge raindrops splattered the stone pathway leading across my front yard. I yelped and shoved my phone into the front pocket of my hoodie to protect it, then yanked on the car's doorhandle.

It didn't budge.

I tapped on the window. The rain fell quicker, soaking my shoulders and the top of my head. Gideon held his phone to his ear and leaned across the seat to unlock the passenger door.

He didn't acknowledge me when I plopped inside like a wet dog, bearing gifts of fatty, sodium-packed snacks.

"Month-to-month," he said. "That's right. I understand it's more expensive. Thank you. I will tell your superior that you went above and beyond."

Gideon tapped the phone and slid it into the center console beneath the radio. The blue light on the AC glowed, a signal to ensure the Civic stayed icy cold. I shivered and pulled on the strings attached to the hood to block the chilly air from freezing my neck.

"I can't tell if you're being sarcastic or not," I said, nodding toward his phone.

His thick brows pressed together, and he grimaced at me. "What is that supposed to mean? I'm never sarcastic. I mean what I say."

Great. So, you meant it when you said it was a mistake to kiss me. Why did I care? He was leaving. I was a criminal. This was ten times worse than the distrust between me and my ex, considering my lifestyle put Gideon's job on the line.

"I didn't realize you could be that nice," I said with a shrug. It was petty, but the storm coupled with the icy car soured my positivity.

"I'm extremely nice," he said. With that, he eased the car from the curb and followed the dirt road out of the rural neighborhood.

"Right," I said, folding my arms to preserve my body heat. "Nice is almost arresting an innocent shop owner because you're frustrated you can't find the thief."

Fox in a henhouse. I needed to keep my mouth shut, but I couldn't help it. Gideon enraged me. He was impossible to understand, emotionless, too focused on his job, and he didn't have the first clue about the significance of Folklore Falls. Once he left, he'd be out of sight and out of mind. I hoped.

Gideon glanced at me, then snapped his head back to the windshield. A flash of white lit up over the falls. Once the sky fell dark again, he grunted.

"You know I looked up those names. I can't find a record of these people anywhere."

I tensed, but didn't let it show on my face. "I wouldn't be surprised if Brett has a fake identification operation going too."

Okay. Brett was a punk and my former bully, but I was digging too deep into the blame against him. Unfortunately, it was too late to stop.

We pulled into the archery range, and I shot Gideon a look. He pursed his lips and raised his brows.

"We can't park outside the estate."

"I thought stakeouts happened in cars," I said, swirling my finger around. Raindrops raced down the windshield, and the steady flow created a white noise effect against the top of the car. It was soothing, pretty even, unless you had to go out into it.

"I hope you brought an umbrella," he said. Gideon kicked his door open and left me alone in the car. My jaw dropped. It wouldn't hurt to get a little wet, but this was not how I imagined our night going. I'd hoped to stay dry, have the Jensens spot us watching them, and ultimately force them to call off the meeting I suspected was intended to move the dagger. Tomorrow, we'd attend the Gala, find the dagger, and Gideon would have his evidence.

I scrambled out into the rain and tromped through the mud to catch up with him. Gideon thrust his arm out to balance the umbrella over both of us. He shifted to walk closer to me, and the heat of his body sent electricity up my arms. Or was it the remnants of the storm?

Another crack of lightning brightened the sky and stabbed the earth somewhere beyond the Jensens' mansion.

"This is dangerous," I said, shouting over the wind and rainfall.

Gideon nodded. "I want you to turn back."

No way.

The sky lit up again, flashing with a white so bright I had to shut my eyes. I was determined, but not stupid. *No way* quickly turned into *let's get the car,* and it wasn't even for my own interests to put the pressure on the Jensen's. I voted ugly beige car stakeout over drowned rats huddling on the edge of the estate to protect us, not just to help the Jensens spot us. Though, I needed them to keep the dagger on the premises until the Gala.

"Come with me," I said, grabbing his arm. Another bolt of lightning cracked, but it didn't slow him.

He shot me a look and shook his head. "I've got a job to do."

"At the risk of your life?" I dug my fingers into his forearm, and he finally stopped and turned to meet my gaze.

"You would know," he said. A thunderous roll deafened the last word, but I gleaned it based on the shape of his mouth. I chewed on my lip and considered his meaning.

I shook my head.

"You're as much a workaholic as I am," he said, nodding down the road as if the B and B were right there. "With your two jobs."

Was that how he saw me? If my jaw could drop any further, I'd have a beard of mud. He knew nothing about me. I worked hard, sure, but I wasn't my job or my degree or even just a thief.

"What does that have to do with anything?"

Gideon pulled his arm from my grasp and shoved the umbrella and his car keys at me until I took them. He turned and continued walking. The wet ground squished with every step as rain splashed and soaked his dark waves.

I let out a sound of frustration and followed him. "Tell me what the hell that's supposed to mean."

He shrugged and wiped the hair that had fallen into his eye. His determined march, tensed jaw, and muddied pants and shoes reminded me of a soldier.

"You need to get where it's safe," he said.

"I can make my own decisions," I snapped back. "Just come with me. We'll get the car and hold the stakeout from there."

"They can't know we're watching."

Quite the contrary. I wanted them to see us, but not as much as I wanted to avoid getting fried by a bolt from the heavens. And if what some religions say about striking down sinners was true, I'd be first in line to get zapped by an angry god.

Gideon continued his aggressive march toward the estate, and I followed tentatively. The gate came into view, a perfect haunting black iron entrance on a stormy evening.

"You're being stupid," I shouted. "What is so important about your job that it's worth your life?"

His shoulders tensed. "Go back," he said without looking back.

"Not without you!"

I shivered. The desperation in my voice might have embarrassed me in any other situation. But this wasn't the time for modesty. I cared about the idiot, and he was marching to his death over a dumb larceny case. I wasn't even stealing anymore.

"You can't get demoted if you're dead," I said.

Gideon stopped and swiveled. His clothes clung to him, and he looked the same as he did in Baird's cave.

"Go to the car," he growled.

"No." Okay. Now I was being stupid, too. But I couldn't leave him there, and what did he care if I had two jobs?

Gideon grunted and stomped toward me. He stopped a hair's breadth away and suddenly crouched.

"What the—"

He wrapped his arms around my legs and forced me over his shoulder.

Oh, hell no!

I kicked and demanded he put me down, but nothing stopped his Darth Vader march. Gideon carried me all the way back to the car and dropped me into the back seat. The open umbrella had pooled water when upside down that splashed over the cloth seat.

I kept my fist tight around the collar of his shirt so he couldn't straighten and ditch me alone in the car.

"What is your problem?" I asked, tugging on his shirt and forcing him halfway into the car.

Gideon shook his head and met my gaze. "You're impossible to understand."

"Me?"

"Look," he said, "I came here to solve this case, not let some sheriff's assistant get under my skin."

I furrowed my brows. "So, we're solving the case. Tomorrow, we'll find what he's stolen, then you can be on your merry way and forget all about Folklore Falls."

He'd get stuck with his head to the side if he didn't stop shaking it at everything I said. "I'm not leaving."

"What?"

Lightning struck close enough to snap our attention away from one another. The rumble of thunder followed immediately after.

"Get inside," I said. He finally listened and pulled the door shut.

"I'm going to follow this case to the end," he said. "And I like it here."

I raised my eyebrows. He stared ahead while I searched his face for clues. The bulge at his jaw broke his stoic expression and revealed he gritted his teeth.

Finally, he turned and met my gaze, dark eyes catching the glow of another flash in the sky.

"I'll be around for a while," he said.

"So, why the rush to solve this tonight?" I asked. Water dripped down my spine from my hair, sending goosebumps all over my body. I reached up and pinched the claw to let my hair fall.

He sighed and looked forward again, watching the rain race down the windshield from our spot in the back seat.

"I've been unprofessional enough," he said. "It's time I redeem myself."

My heart dropped into my stomach. Not this again. The kiss was one moment, and yet, he dwelled on it like it'd wrecked his whole life.

"Nobody knows about that."

Gideon's gaze dropped to his lap, then trailed back up to meet mine. "You do."

My pulse sped to match the rapid pelting of the rain on the car's roof. I swallowed and licked my lips. He not only trusted me, he worried what I thought, and based on his determination to get me into the car and a place of safety, he cared about me, too. I wanted to lean in, but all courage left me. All the fire I felt while screaming and kicking at him to put me down faded to a flicker, a tense, thready flame that hinged on what he'd do next.

"Look." He frowned, and the scar bent and twisted. "When my fiancée died, I couldn't focus. I lost all credibility at my job and let grief distract me. I took this case to prove I was still a good cop." He sighed and raked his fingers through his hair, pressing the wet waves against his head. "And then I met you."

"I'm—" I stopped, not knowing what to say. Should I apologize? What did I have to do with any of this? I wanted to say sorry for the loss of his fiancée but couldn't find my voice to speak up again. He'd listened to me. It was my time to return the favor.

"You're focused and good at your job," he said. "It wasn't right of me to interfere. I just thought, I—" his voice trailed, and he took a tentative breath, glancing away, then back at me. "You spoke so passionately about the legend. I never thought it was possible to believe stories like that, and it fascinated me. I'm black and white on everything, but this felt…" He shrugged. "Gray."

A sudden laugh escaped me. He really was horrible with compliments. Gideon pinched his brows, and his lips parted as he searched my face.

"I'm sorry," I said, biting my smile back down. His confession filled me with a million feelings, from nerves to guilt to warmth. "Gray is an awful color. It's almost as bad as beige."

His confusion deepened with a crease on his forehead.

"Never mind—"

"You left the case," he said before the subject changed. "I crossed the line of professionalism, and you dropped the case. It's on me. I own that, but it shouldn't be at the expense of your job."

My stomach twisted. All the butterflies inside me choked and died at that last word. This wasn't my job. I wasn't a sheriff's assistant—not even close. Everything Gideon knew about me was a lie. Everything except the pieces of truth I'd allowed him to see, like my passion for Folklore Falls's history.

Now he planned to stay, which meant he'd eventually learn the truth. Gideon was too smart and too good for me to stay under his radar forever. I didn't want him to leave, but I needed it.

"You don't have to protect me," I said. It was selfish of me to let him worry about my nonexistent police station job.

"I do," he said.

"No, you don't understand—"

"I'm confident you can protect yourself," Gideon said, interrupting me. He shifted in the seat to face me. The space between us was as nonexistent as my law enforcement career. "But it's just the way I am. I couldn't protect my fiancée from the drunk driver who killed her, so I go overboard."

Rain showered the car in a steady stream. My gaze flickered to his mouth, but he misunderstood.

"Yes," he said, "the scar is from the accident."

I couldn't help myself. Before I knew what I was doing, I reached out and brushed my thumb over the jagged line of flesh. But the scar wasn't my focus. I wanted an excuse to touch him.

"I didn't leave the case because you kissed me," I said. The words slipped out before I could stop myself. He deserved as much honesty as I could give him. "Gideon." I took a shaky breath and shifted to face him. The heat had masked the cold from my wet clothes. "I'm not Sheriff Max's assistant."

"What?"

The disappointment in his voice caused bile to rise in my throat. I swallowed, but my tongue already tasted bitter.

"I'm doing community service because I destroyed property at the resort." My heart skipped a beat. It didn't sound like the words came from my mouth. I felt like the puppet now, though his Oscar the Grouch expression returned. "Sheriff Max knows I'm observant and that I know everybody in town, so he thought I could help you. I'm really sorry I didn't make this clear to you."

The knot in his throat bobbed, and the sword scar vanished into a deep frown.

"I'm so sorry," I repeated, wishing it could wipe the disappointment and pain of betrayal from his face. I'd been here before. I'd driven the man I cared about away because of lies and secrets. *Better off alone.* "I'm—I'm not always honest. You wouldn't like who I—"

Gideon took a deep breath and shifted his jaw. "This back and forth between us. Was that a lie, too?"

I chewed on my lip, my heart pounding. One butterfly squeezed out from beneath the rock in my stomach and fluttered in my chest again. Gideon could never know the full truth. Never. But a strange relief flooded me as he'd asked about the tension between us rather than the job. Once again, he subverted my expectations. Maybe his job wasn't his sole focus in life.

"Not for me," I whispered.

"So, I didn't put your job on the line?" he asked. I shook my head and forced myself to hold his gaze. I deserved to feel all the guilt and to process the hurt in his eyes. Except his pinched expression relaxed with my response, and I could have sworn I saw the hint of a smile at one corner of his mouth.

Gideon cursed. "I don't understand you at all."

"I'm really—"

Before I could say sorry again, Gideon's mouth found mine. His fingers threaded through my wet hair at the bottom of my neck and all breath left my lungs. The butterfly buzzed, then froze as I opened my mouth and tasted him again.

I traced my tongue over the top of his mouth and gasped as his hands dropped from the back of my head to my hips and he pulled me into him. My body pressed against his wet clothes. He groaned when I bit his lip, and a rush of delight rippled through me at the sound. His teeth gently swept over my bottom lip as he returned the favor.

He trusts you, Loxley. Guilt nagged me, but sensations took hold of me. The minty and salty taste of him crowded the thought away, and the pressure of his fingers tightening around my hips clouded my mind.

We caught our breaths just long enough for him to speak.

"I love…" he paused. "Holding you."

I cupped his face and kissed him again.

Another flash of light brightened everything outside the car. I let him pull me into his lap. We laughed, breathless and quick, as his elbow hit the side of the car and the top of my head bumped into the ceiling. It only lasted a moment before my hands found his jawline, then the back of his head, through his hair. I couldn't bring him close enough to me, and I wanted to elicit that groan of delight again.

How the hell did this happen? The thought dissipated with that sound.

He was a cop, and I, the thief he hunted. Except for tonight.

Right now, we were two people caught in a storm—caught up in each other.

I wasn't a criminal or a liar or the financial supplier for Folklore Falls's people in need. With our fingers tangled in each other's hair, it broke us down to the basics, two people—opposite people—drawn to one another.

Just Loxley and Gideon.

Nineteen

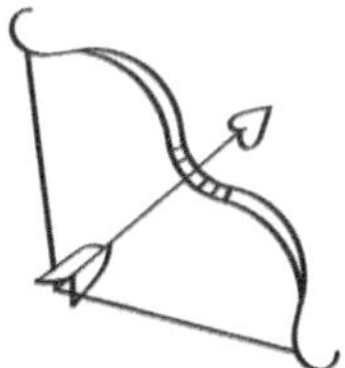

Nobody dared drive in the storm. Or at least we never spotted headlights or a car turning down the road to the Jensens. Of course, in our heated state of distraction and the flash of lightning, we could have missed the meeting.

I splashed cold water on my face, hoping to shrink my pores before applying makeup. Thought that was one myth I believed less likely than Grayson Baird marrying a faery. It never worked, but I had zero desire to spend my hard-earned money on the fancy makeup of the elite, so I used whatever tricks I could find to match them when I needed to fit in.

Tonight, I'd attend the Gala among both the vacationers and the residents, but I wasn't worried about tricking or impressing them.

Last night, Gideon and I had both distracted one another from our goals, and it was worth it. But it meant we needed to stay focused and sharp at the Gala, not letting a single smile or shared gaze cloud our thoughts. He'd be counting on using the opportunity to find the tool and watch the Jensens while I planned to find the dagger.

I had to hope the rumors I'd spread were enough for the Jensens to call off the meeting and not risk moving the dagger.

A knock came at the door, and I let out a curse. It'd better not be Gideon. He was an early bird, and it drove me nuts.

I hurried through my house and swung the door open. Grandpa Owl smiled.

"Sorry it took so long, Little Robin," he said.

"What did?" I asked, scrunching up my face. A pile of ruby fabric was folded in his hands. He extended his arms and nodded for me to take it. "What's this?"

"A project I started earlier this week," he said. He beamed brighter than the porch light shining off his bald head. "It even has pockets."

I lifted the fabric, and it unfolded in a waterfall of shimmering red. The dress was simple, just the way I liked it, but classy, with a sweetheart neckline and sleeves that'd cling to the edges of my shoulders. Grandpa Owl designed it to be modest as any grandfather would, but he'd made it captivating in a different way with the silky fabric catching light and the skirt expanding in width, starting from the knees. Betty the Betta would appreciate the mermaid style.

I chewed on my lip and met Grandpa Owl's gaze. It was then I noticed he wore a suit and a black tie.

"Wow," I said, smiling. "You look wonderful!"

Grandpa Owl looked away, smiling with modesty.

"You have a date, don't you?" I asked.

He cleared his throat and shuffled his feet. "I wouldn't call it a date." He bent to wipe off imaginary dirt from his shiny shoes. "I'm accompanying Diana to the Gala. Since I've been through the grief she's experiencing now, I thought I'd offer companionship."

I invited Grandpa inside and offered him a cup of tea. He meandered into the kitchen and insisted on brewing a cup for himself. Apparently, the process gave him courage. It was sweet to see my grandfather full of nerves over his date with Diana.

"Speaking of dates," he called from the kitchen. I'd shut myself in the bathroom to slip on the dress. It fit, and I wouldn't even have to hold my breath or wiggle out of it for fear of ripping the fabric. I popped small hoop earrings with fake red jewels lining the hoop like planets on a solar ring, then gathered half of my hair and twisted it into the claw for a purposefully loose bun. After pulling a lock of hair from the claw to hang down either side of my face, I smirked at myself in the mirror, knowing my teenage self would appreciate the early 2000s style.

When I opened the bathroom door, Grandpa Owl repeated himself.

"What about them?" I danced back into the kitchen on one foot while I slipped a black-heeled sandal on the other.

"You and Gideon," he said without more explanation. The tea kettle whistled as if on cue, and Grandpa smirked.

"There is no me and Gideon." *Lie.* Last night was all about me and Gideon in the backseat with more me and Gideon in my dreams after he'd dropped me back at home early this morning. I suppressed a smile at the memory.

Grandpa Owl fixed my tea first in a mug Bella had gifted me. I fastened the strap on my shoe and accepted the cup that said *Bows Before Bros* with an arrow beneath the words.

"I don't know if you realize that I've become quite good friends with Officer Notting lately."

It was no surprise, considering Grandpa Owl made friends with everyone who stayed at Sherwood Bed and Breakfast. But Gideon didn't exactly invite conversation with his eternal grump face and folded arms. I smirked, remembering how I couldn't see his frown if my mouth was on his. Though, I liked the brooding expression now. He reminded me of a tortured vigilante, an anti-hero bearing scars while he saved the world under his strict set of rules.

I sipped the peppermint tea and appreciated that the flavor would freshen my breath. Though, tonight was about the dagger, not Gideon.

When I said nothing, Grandpa Owl continued. "Gideon has changed since he arrived a few weeks back. Why do you think that is?" He took a victory sip of the tea and sat across from me at the small, round table.

I knew what he wanted me to say, but I wasn't like him or Diana— I didn't long for companionship.

"For someone who arrived here with a single-minded purpose, he sure talks about you a lot."

"That's because I've been helping him with the case," I said. "Gideon is obsessed with his job."

"And I'm the king of Folklore Falls." He chuckled.

I rolled my eyes and polished off the mug of warmth before standing and reminding him he had a date to get to. With the tea mugs discarded in the sink, we made our way to the entry. Gideon would arrive to pick me up any moment, which meant I needed to shuffle Grandpa Owl out and to my neighbor's before I felt like an embarrassed teen going to prom again.

Too late.

Gideon stood on my porch. His suit didn't quite fit, revealing he'd bought or borrowed it at the last minute. It was too short at the ankles, and I assumed the arms too, but he'd unbuttoned the surgeon's cuffs on the sleeves and rolled both the suit and white shirt sleeves halfway up his forearms. The tossed look of his hair gave the appearance he'd tried to style it, but the breeze knocked it back into his face, where he brushed it out of his eyes.

"Hi," I said, unable to find any other words.

The smile that encompassed his face filled my chest with warmth. Or maybe peppermint triggered my acid reflux, though I couldn't remember the last time I had heartburn. I expected the uncertainty of locating the dagger, carrying the weight of my lies, and the struggles of the entire town on my shoulders to tip off my anxiety and build up the acid reflux, but I remained calm.

"Hey," he said. His eyes shifted to the movement behind me. "Mr. Cameron." Gideon nodded at Grandpa Owl.

I chewed my lip. The remnants of peppermint and honey lingered on my tongue, but the taste of Gideon's mouth took over my memory. I blinked away from staring at his lips. Even in the absence of my grandfather, kissing was inappropriate. We had a job to do. Two, in fact, with one that I needed to keep a secret from the person I was dying to tell.

"I was just leaving." Grandpa Owl squeezed my arm as he passed, then patted Gideon on the shoulder. Once my grandfather was out of earshot, Gideon turned to me and raised his eyebrows.

He took a deep breath, raking his eyes over my body, then landing his gaze back on mine. "If I compliment you, will you accept it?"

I exhaled into a half-laugh and scrunched my nose. "Probably not." Before he could say something silly in his Gideon-speak, I spoke again and stepped over the threshold. "But I know you're capable of normal compliments."

"Yeah?" he said.

My hand lingered on the doorknob after pulling the door shut. He didn't move to allow me more space on the porch, and we stood inches apart. The heat from his body and the familiar scent of sandalwood brought me back to last night. The ground was wet and white tufts of pollen clung to grass and dirt and everything after being blown around.

"You called the falls stunning," I said, meeting his eyes again.

He smirked, doing that vanishing act with the scar again. "And it still doesn't compare to you."

I bit my lip and refused to let the heat rise from my chest to my face. "Wow," I said with a nod. "That's good. You're getting better."

"Let's see if I can bring that improvement to the job too," he said. Gideon raised his hand as if to say 'after you.' The tension shriveled at his mention of the case. We'd shared an intimate moment last night, but it didn't change the situation.

"Bye Betty," I mumbled.

"What was that?" Gideon asked, opening the passenger car door for me.

"Oh, nothing. It's dumb."

"You can tell me." He jogged to the other door and looked at me from across the top of the small car.

"I always say goodbye to my fish when I leave to house. It's my little ritual." I sucked in a cleansing breath and climbed into his car.

"And you tease me for hanging my shoes up." He chuckled.

I socked him in the arm. "Hey! It makes the house feel less empty is all."

Gideon smiled and I found my gaze dropping to his lips then trace the scar and up his jawline. I chewed my lip.

"I didn't mean to tease," he said.

"Oh, don't worry. I may embarrass myself by saying goodbye to a fish, but that's nothing compared to being whipped at a game of darts in front of the whole town." I smirked.

Gideon's smile sent electricity throughout my body and it took everything I had not to reach across the center console and pull his face to mine. Of course, that'd be dangerous considering he'd already pulled away from the curb.

I shot a quick text to Bella, who'd agreed to be my discreet lookout at the party. Or at least, I assumed her cheeky response was an agreement.

Can my lookout be on Brett and only Brett? Because I can't promise my eyes won't be glued to him. But then if he opens his mouth I might punch him. Such a shame that a gorgeous man like that has a garbage personality.

She hated the guy as much as I did, but that never stopped her from admiring his rear end.

During the drive, Gideon and I discussed the plans. We'd share a dance, mingle, enjoy a non-alcoholic drink to stay sharp, and with small splits in between each action.

"That will give me time to slip away and locate the tool or stolen objects," I said, shuffling through the pictures of the jewelry, statues, and other items I'd taken. Gideon provided the photographs to give me a visual and help me find them. Though I had already sold these through the pawnshop, Johnny kept that out of the records and Gideon in the dark. The backwardness of it all ignited the burning sensation in my throat and chest. Acid reflux had returned.

I shoved the guilt into the back of my mind and listened to Gideon.

"While you're," he paused, "looking around, I'll aim for a chance to speak with each of the Jensens separately."

I nodded, glancing out the window at the archery range as we drove past. The reflection of my face in the glass revealed my cheeks flushed pink. The range was once my escape, a place to go let off steam or practice for a tournament and get my mind off the financial troubles in town. Now, the memory of our time together changed it to a place of passion.

I felt Gideon's eyes on me, so I kept mine staring forward as we turned onto the Jensens' road.

"You know, to glean information based on their behavior and reactions," he explained.

I arched my eyebrow and shot him a look. "I might not be a cop, but I got what you meant."

Cars lined the sides of the dirt road that had turned to mud with the rain. I appreciated that the Jensens had kept their private road with the style of the town and put-off paving it, but today it'd ruin a lot of shoes.

"I'm sorry," he said with a slight shrug. "That was petty. If I'm honest, I'm still troubled by the deception."

I closed my eyes and swallowed a lump in my throat. It stoked the fire in my chest.

"Are you okay?" he asked.

My eyes shot open, and I nodded, taking a huge, shaking breath. "Yeah, yes. I'm focused on the plan." *Lie.* I couldn't stop thinking about last night—about how we'd let our guards down, yet I was still tricking him.

Vacationers and townsfolk alike emerged from their vehicles and hiked toward the open iron gate. Inside, the grounds were manicured, and the cobblestone driveway created a rainbow effect of brown, white, and gray.

This felt gray. Gideon's weird comment came back to me. I was in a gray area. I lived my life there, not good, not bad—just a criminal who breaks the law to help others. I was on the other side of the rock when you pick it up from the earth and turn it over to find mud and worms clinging to it.

People stood in groups, already receiving hors d'oeuvres and flutes of a bubbling golden beverages. Some chatted in the gardens among statues and fountains, while others made their way to the building or stood gossiping on the porch between the white columns that made the place look like it housed the president.

Two greeters dressed in black and white attire held the double doors open wide and smiled as we approached or whenever another guest stepped across the threshold. The remnant glow of the sunset caught the colors of the stained-glass ceiling and painted the entryway with a rainbow brighter than the arch of the driveway.

Gideon tentatively cupped my elbow as we climbed the front steps, and my unpracticed gait while wearing heels had me walking like Bambi. If I dropped my hand and laced my fingers through his, it'd solidify our undercover status, right?

Instead, I brought my hand to my face and swiped away the dangling hair that had blown out and stuck to my glossy lips.

I spied Grandpa Owl and Diana in the hallway, admiring the paintings. On the staircase stood Brett Jensen, another man with a permanent scowl. Though, he didn't trigger a burst of butterflies in me. Brett looked irritated each time anyone opened their mouths, then he downed an entire glass of red wine in one gulp.

The other Jensen brother had his arm laced around his wife's waist. She held the hand of their son, whose suit looked twelve times more expensive than Gideon's even though the child would outgrow it in a year.

Doctor Jensen, the patriarch of the family, greeted everyone who walked in the door with a smile that I couldn't pick apart. I wanted to claim it fake, but he looked genuinely pleased with each person's arrival. With every guest, he engaged personally while Mrs. Jensen white-knuckled a champagne glass and kept her lips sealed.

I was dying to ask why they'd held the Gala here rather than at the resort itself, but I didn't need to draw attention to the fact that I wanted to case their property.

To the right, doors opened into a ballroom where guests enjoyed live music. I took in everything, using the skill Gideon claimed I had— the skill I'd honed as a thief.

I knew where I could stand to pop the glittering waterfall broach off Mrs. Jensen's women's suit. I spied a pathway among the dancing that'd lead me past the richest guests, who, no doubt, had watches, necklaces, and wallets within reach.

A warm hand took mine, and I gasped. Lost in the moment, I didn't expect Gideon to interrupt. He stared at me, his eyes telling me he knew I was doing my part.

He leaned into my ear and whispered. "A dance first, right?"

I nodded. The natural movement of assimilating with the other guests was key, not unlike my "focus" on the gossip and games at the resort's casino.

Neither of us claimed a talent for dancing, but our bodies moved easily together. His hand dropped to my waist, and I wanted his fingers gripped around my hip bone like last night. I needed him closer, yet out of my way, so I could see when Brett moved off the stairs. I'd start with the upstairs safe, then make my way back down toward the cellar.

Gideon kept his eyes on me, watching for my signal. We moved slowly, and I silently thanked the string quartet for dropping the pace of the song, so we didn't stick out in the crowd.

My heart skipped a beat as his hand slipped over the curve of my butt. Gideon coughed and cleared his throat, quickly moving his grip back to my waist. But he held me closer during the slow song, squeezing tighter with every step.

The guests, jewelry, even the dagger muted around me. I found myself observing Gideon's mouth and trying to discern the meaning in his focused expression. Dark eyes fixed on me, and my breath left as he leaned closer. With his face an inch away, my lips parted.

I wanted him to say it again. *I love holding you.*

Gideon opened his mouth, and my heart skipped a beat. "Is he alone?" he asked, his voice low and husky.

I blinked. "What?"

"Brett Jensen," he whispered.

I sucked in air to catch my breath and tilted my head to gain sight past the doors and toward the grand staircase.

"Yes," I said.

"I guess that means I have to let go." His hands moved to my hips, and his fingers lingered in the same place they'd squeezed when I climbed on top of him last night.

The song ended, and all the tension left me breathless and distracted. It dissipated the moment Gideon released his hold on me.

"Remember the photographs," he said. "Good luck."

Right. I nodded and chewed on my lip.

This was why I didn't want a date to the Gala. I needed to focus and use my one opportunity to move freely about the Jensen estate.

Always better off alone.

Twenty

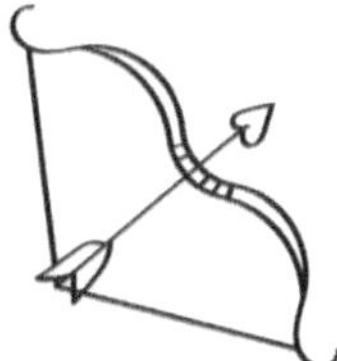

The density of the crowd made my investigation easier than expected. I moved without suspicion, making for the staircase.

Closed doors caught my eye, and I paused on the first step. With one hand on the banister, I balanced precariously on the edge of the step and furrowed my brows. Every other door on this floor was wide open, like an invitation for all to admire each inch of expensive furniture and decor.

I glanced around the entry and spied Gideon edging his way to Brett, who knocked back another glass of wine. At least he'd be easy to talk with after consuming all that alcohol.

Once I confirmed each guest was engaged in conversation, I lifted my chin at Bella. From the corner of the room she returned the faint nod. I spun back to the closed doors and slipped into the shadow of the staircase. The doors were locked, but I didn't have any trouble taking a pin from my hair and bending it to fit through the hole in the doorknob.

The latched clicked, and I turned the knob. I didn't dare turn on the light, but moved with the illumination of the moon streaming in through large windows on either side of the study.

A desk sat in the middle of the room, with massive bookshelves lining the wall behind it. I tiptoed over the rug and raked my eyes over small statues, leather-bound books, trophies, and an ax on the wall.

Of course, this tool was intact, not the same one used to break through Baird's hiding place. I almost expected to see the dagger on display, along with the other odd objects.

The buzz of conversation wafted in from the crack under the doors. I held my breath and crouched to check under the desk. Nothing looked remotely like a safe or a blade.

I stood and sighed before shoveling through the desk drawers. I paused as a document caught my eye.

Re-zoning Folklore Falls.

"What the hell?" I whispered, tracing my finger under the words to speed-read. My heart thumped faster with every sentence. Nothing mentioned the dagger, but the document was a far worse threat to my town.

A cheer rose from beyond the study. The familiar voice of Mayor Richard boomed over everyone else's, and I guessed he'd found a microphone.

Was this the reason they held the Gala at their estate?

3,700 acres re-zoned for commercial purposes. Folklore Falls State Park excluded.

My stomach twisted. I'd accused the Jensens of bullying, carelessness, and greed—but I never thought they'd try to turn the entire town inside out.

I shuffled through papers with my heart pounding. The edge of a document sliced through my thumb. I brought the finger to my lips and sucked the blood away, but didn't stop until I found what I'd suspected.

The Jensens planned to buy the entire town. But how would they get approval to re-zone?

My heart dropped to my stomach. I snapped my head up and held my breath, listening carefully to Mayor Richard's speech. My phone buzzed in my pocket, but I ignored it, straining to hear the mayor's voice.

"I'll be stepping down earlier than my term prescribes—"

No...

"But I'd like to welcome you to my vote for next in office—"

No.

"Mr. Thomas Jensen!"

Like a lifted veil, it all became clear. Mr. Jensen had greeted everyone because this wasn't a party, it was a campaign. He'd run the town, re-zone everything, and buy it, all with the help of the dagger's profit.

Classy clapping drowned out Mr. Jensen's hellos in the microphone. Of course they hosted the campaign at their estate because it put on the face of the friendly neighbor. If Folklore Fall's residents loved anything, it was a friendly neighbor.

Emotion caught in my throat. Bile rose and burned my esophagus. I nearly puked all over the Cherrywood desk.

This was beyond my jurisdiction. I'd need Gideon's help.

"I can't use him," I said, my voice splitting the silence of the room. The sound startled me, as if it hadn't come from my mouth. I argued with myself, knowing what I needed but unable to push past the sick feeling.

I'd already lied to him and put his job on the line. I refused to use him, too. But maybe he'd understand. Maybe I could come clean with this evidence to show him how much the Jensens will hurt Folklore Falls.

He'd understood the gray area, right?

The burning resided from my throat but remained firm in my chest. Anxiety had me chewing on the flesh of my thumb now rather than sucking the blood from the paper cut.

Gideon had trusted me. It was time to trust him. The thought silenced everything else. I stopped chewing, my pulse slowed, and I almost felt excited. I wanted him to know the truth. I wanted him to know *me*.

I finally had a real reason to risk everything and come clean.

GIDEON

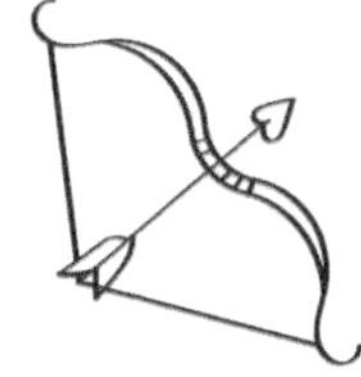

I t took everything I had to tear my eyes away from Loxley and find Brett Jensen. She balanced on the stairs like a bird on a branch, beautiful, and seeing everything but without the skittish energy. Loxley moved with confidence yet remained inconspicuous, without the demand for attention, like most of the others in the room.

I forced myself to focus and excused my way past groups of minglers. Brett stood beside his brother and spoke with another couple opposite them.

"Hello," I said, trying to fix my face from the grouchy expression Loxley always accused me of. I thrust out my hand in a way that demanded Brett shake it. "I wanted to congratulate you and your family on the renovations done on the resort."

Brett grunted and offered me a limp hand. Now I saw what Loxley meant. A permanent scowl was off-putting. Especially on a person as tall and as broad-shouldered as Brett Jensen. I stood an inch or two above the average height for a man, but Brett towered over me, a sore thumb in a crowd of paper-thin women and wealthy men who'd never labored a day in their lives.

"Hey," the woman from the other couple spoke in a shrieking voice. "Is that the girl from the bed-and-breakfast?"

Her husband frowned and squinted. "The psycho that tried to steal your ring? Yeah, that's her."

My ears pricked, and I snapped my head to follow the direction of their gaze. Loxley lifted her chin at someone across the room, and my watch ping-ponged to the woman who responded from the other side. I knew that face.

I grit my teeth and stared until she looked right at me.

The girl from the pawnshop.

"What did you say?" I spun back and interrupted the couples' conversation about property prices and how that'd all soon change. The couple sounded interested in buying acreage in Folklore Falls. Brett stood, a silent, looming statue but forgotten by me—for now.

"Excuse me, who are you?" the shrieking woman asked with an upturned lip.

"Someone who can help if you suffered the loss of a valuable," I said.

"We got it back," her husband said lazily, with a thumb pointed to his wife's hand.

"Wait," the woman spoke again, causing my ears to ring with the high pitch of her voice. She turned to her husband and slapped a palm over her chest. The giant diamond on her hand glittered by catching the glow of the chandelier. It looked nearly identical to the one Loxley had worn a time or two. "Did you ever consider maybe you didn't lose that chunk of cash? What if *she* took it out of your wallet? It was the same day it went missing."

I furrowed my brows and darted my attention back to the husband to gauge his reaction. He parted his lips, but his eyebrows didn't move.

"Maybe," he said, nodding.

When I looked back to the staircase, Loxley was gone. I felt the weight of eyes on me, but it wasn't the couple, or Brett. I scanned the crowd and trailed the source back to the woman from the pawnshop. I racked my brain to recall her name, Belle, or Brianna, or something. Loxley rarely spoke about the two at the pawnshop.

She averted her eyes with the quick snap of her head in another direction. Why had she been watching me? And why nod to Loxley?

The crowd shifted, pushing me away from Brett and the couples as everyone looked to the ballroom. A skinny man had taken a microphone from somewhere and stood on the stage beside the musicians. He introduced himself as Mayor Richard, a man I had yet to meet because he was always absent from the town he claimed to run.

I flicked my gaze back to the corner, not wanting to lose sight of the woman possibly working with Loxley. She stared at her phone, tapping away at the screen, then shot her eyes back up to me. Everyone else stood still, waiting for the mayor's next words. Belle, or whoever she was, pushed against the crowd as they rose their hands to clap at the announcement followed by Mr. Jensen's full name.

"Wait," I said, as if she could hear me. Loxley had admitted to me she wasn't honest. She *told* me I wouldn't like her, but I didn't listen.

I shoved through the crowd. Belle picked up her pace and almost made it to the open doors when I grabbed her wrist and pulled her into the empty hallway. The people had gathered around the ballroom to hear the announcement, which left the branching halls clear.

"No, I don't want to dance." She yanked her hand away from me.

"You're a friend of Loxley's," I said. The threads connected, but the only words that came out were simple and nearly useless.

"No."

"Don't lie. You're not as good at it as she is." Rage built in my chest as confusion melted away. Pain mingled with the anger, and I didn't know whether to punch the wall or knock my head against it. I'd been manipulated.

Belle's jaw nearly unhinged. She glanced across the room to where Loxley had stood.

"What is she really doing here?" I asked.

"You already know," she said, "locating the dagger."

"She didn't steal that, too?" I curled my hands into fists.

Belle laughed suddenly and twisted her eyebrows in disbelief. "This is a joke. Loxley wants nothing more than to see that dagger in a museum. She's the only barrier between the vacationers destroying this town."

"By stealing?"

Belle opened her mouth, but I didn't want to hear the answer. My short fingernails dug into my palms, and I pushed past her. The single-minded focus blinded me to my surroundings, and I crashed into the only other person moving through the crowd.

Brett snarled an apology, and I glanced back to watch him storm down the same hallway I'd left Belle.

I shook my head and pressed through the crowd. I'd find Loxley before she stole anything else, and I'd put her in handcuffs for once and for all.

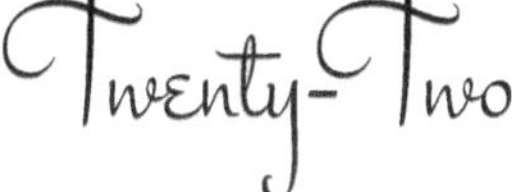

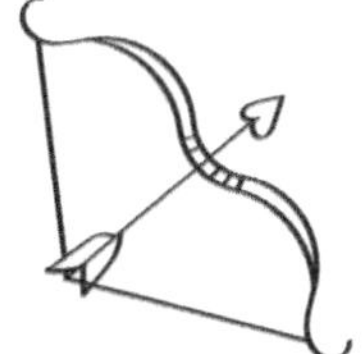

FFICER NOTTING KNOWS AND HE'S GOING TO ARREST YOU! GET OUT NOW!

A million emotions slammed me at once from a single text message. I heaved, the acid reflux coming back full swing and dragging anxiety, disappointment, and shame with it. The worst part was that Gideon knew I'd lied.

I shoved the phone back in my pocket and scrambled to bring the papers with me. Fight or flight had me running like a chicken for the window. Something gray caught my eye at the bottom corner of the bookshelf.

I froze. Wedged between two stacks of classic French novels was a gray tome too large to be a normal book. Mayor Richard's voice echoed, and I glanced at the door.

The crowd would hold off Gideon for a moment or two. I knelt and turned the book over to see it had no markings but a dial on the other side.

It only exists in a book. The words from the man at the casino came back to me. I was right all along. Brett Jensen took the dagger and hid it on his property.

I exhaled, closed my eyes, and brought my ear to the dial. Listening for the contact points in the lever, I focused and identified the first number, causing the click. But it would take too long, hours even—not moments.

I stood, pushed the screen off the window, hefted the small safe under my arm, and swung my leg outside. Everything felt wrong, from the acid in my throat to the great escape. I didn't have the guts to get arrested. Not yet. I needed to show Gideon the dagger and prove Brett Jensen the bigger criminal. I'd serve my time, eventually. It was impossible to avoid at this point.

Maybe Gideon would understand. It was all that mattered now. He'd never trust me, and we'd never share the intimacy we did last night again.

But maybe he'd forgive me.

The door opened, crashing against the wall with force. Cheers and the white noise of clapping flooded the room. My lungs went flat, devoid of air, though my mouth hung open, gaping at the man I tried to avoid.

Gideon's mouth shaped around my name, but I didn't hear his voice. I couldn't move, couldn't breathe, and couldn't tear my eyes away from him. Pain twisted his face, but it was anger that came from his mouth.

"Stop!" he shouted. He stormed up to me, bringing with him a wave of sandalwood and the salty smell of sweat that brought me back to our heated exchange last night. If only for a second.

Instinct had me scrambling to drag my other leg over the windowsill, but Gideon moved too fast. He gripped my wrist and yanked me halfway back inside. Time spent pickpocketing taught me to move fluidly, and I slipped from his grasp. But the safe weighed me down and took one hand out of the fight. Before I knew it, Gideon grabbed me again and thrust cold metal against my throat with his other hand.

"You tricked me," he said.

"I did." I straightened and moved from straddling the windowsill to facing him. Gideon didn't move the blade from my skin, but his eyes flicked over me, shock apparent on his face.

"And I regret it. But I don't regret helping the people who needed it."

His mouth twitched into a horrible, twisted frown that made his sword scar stab into his chin.

"All this time." His voice lacked the vitriol from earlier. It sounded rough now, breathy and hoarse from shouting. "You were right in front of me."

His dark eyes searched mine, and the pain in them triggered a flood inside me.

"I'm sorry," I said, blinking back tears. I was so close, I had the dagger and I could shut down the Jensens' plan to destroy my hometown. But despite the evidence I held in my arms, the giant hole in my chest told me I'd lost everything. There were no more butterflies, no more burning fire—just emptiness.

Better. Off. Alone.

"Drop the book and turn around," he demanded.

"It's not a book—"

He took the safe from my arms and turned it over.

"It's the dagger. It has to be in there," I scrambled to explain.

"Did you put it there? Are you working with Brett or the other Jensens?" He didn't care to look at the safe, only dropped it on the rug beside us. His dark eyes didn't let me go for a second.

"No!"

Gideon grit his teeth and leaned into my face. Though it was meant to be intimidating, his eyes softened. For a moment, we held one another's gaze, inches away. I swallowed. If he didn't have a weapon at my throat, I might dare to taste him one last time before he threw me in jail. His chin quivered, and his eyes dropped to my mouth. I wasn't the only one sensing the tension and remembering how it felt to be this close to a kiss rather than a threat.

He sighed, pulled the blade back, and opened his fist. The knife clattered against the safe, then fell with a thud on the rug. Every muscle in my body ached and refused to release from rigidity.

Instead of a weapon, Gideon produced another metal object. The handcuffs clinked against one another as he pulled them from his belt.

"Loxley Cameron, you're under the arrest for multiple accounts of grand larceny."

I closed my eyes and waited for the cold metal to slap against my wrist and cover the bow and arrow tattoo. Nothing happened. A heavy silence fell between us, and it felt we existed in a bubble.

"How does the dagger help anyone?" he asked.

I opened my eyes and furrowed my brow. He was willing to listen. He was always willing to listen, and it drew me to him from that first meeting over plates at Fryer Tuck's.

No doubt he felt my pulse pounding against his fingers on my wrist.

"I want to sell it to buy back the businesses that were lost," I said. "It's a gray area."

His jaw shifted."So, you're a criminal." Instead of securing the handcuffs on me, he dropped his hold on my wrist and stepped back. His arms hung limp at his sides.

"What're you doing?" I asked. The heat from his body, and the smell of his breath faded as he put distance between us with another backward step.

"Nobody is just one thing," he said. "At least that's what I'd like to believe."

"What?" The buzz of my phone, mingling bodies beyond on the door, and heavy tension left my head spinning.

"Gray area," he said. With that, he turned and marched for the door. Invisible weight sat on his sagging shoulders, but he walked with determination.

"Wait."

Gideon stopped but didn't afford me the respect of turning around. So, I spoke to his back, and I didn't even deserve that.

"I didn't lie about everything." I wrung my fingers with my other hand, ignoring that I squeezed so hard it hurt. "I never wanted to hurt you."

An indistinguishable sound came from him. Something between a scoff and a laugh.

"I suggest you leave and stay out of my sight," he said. "There's only one cell in this town, and you don't want to share it with Brett Jensen."

I couldn't find the voice to speak again. When Gideon vanished beyond the doors and into the crowd, I turned and climbed from the window.

I left the dagger and, it felt, my heart on the floor of the study.

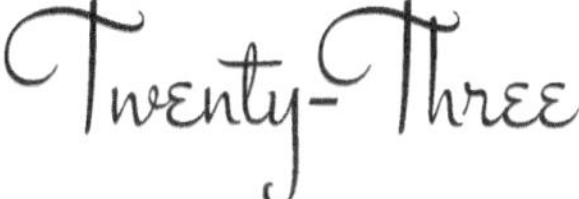

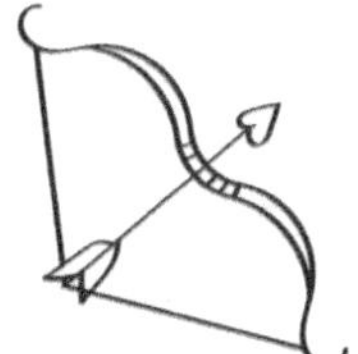

The Jensens never needed the dagger. It was insurance, a backup plan, something they believed they deserved for being the richest family to grow up in Folklore Falls. The resort's reopening drew a bigger crowd than I'd ever seen before, even with the prices doubled.

At least, that was what I picked up from far away. The attic at Sherwood Bed and Breakfast didn't have air conditioning and only one small, round window, but I had my phone to access the outside world. I didn't mind the stuffiness; it was the quiet that got old.

The ache in my back from sleeping on a damaged cot had me hobbling around like an old witch. Mama pretended she didn't know I hid up here, and I preferred it that way. She didn't need to get involved and risk becoming an accomplice if Gideon changed his mind and came for me.

He hadn't. Not yet.

Eleven days passed with me hiding like a coward. I'd called both Johnny and Bella to ensure they'd been left alone. Bella celebrated our former childhood bully's arrest but the joy came with a bittersweet taste when she also couldn't pay rent at the bookstore.

I sat on the floor and leaned against the wall beneath the window.

The sill dug into the back of my neck, but I ignored it. A warm breeze blew through the open window for a breath of fresh air. It stirred up dust around the attic that looked like ghosts when the stream of sunlight caught the white flecks floating—my only company in the empty room.

I pulled the news up on my phone to watch the video of Brett's arrest for the hundredth time. He'd spent exactly twenty-nine minutes in jail before Gideon had realized his mistake—my mistake. Our target was never the youngest son of the Jensen family.

The mother, the matriarch, Mrs. Milan Jensen, came clean after breaking down on national television over her baby boy's arrest. She handed herself over to Gideon in a puddle of tears and apologies to Brett.

The same thought spun in my head for the past eleven days and resurfaced again with the repeated video. *Why do we hurt the people we love the most?*

Mama's frown and misty eyes haunted my mind's eye from the day the Culps dragged their entire family from the B and B. I'd broken her heart while convincing myself it had to be done.

I had to steal to help Diana save her house and Sara finish law school. They'd worked so hard for everything they accomplished, and the elite's greed had ripped it away. Billy needed the bowling alley income to pay for his chemotherapy, and Fryer Tuck would no doubt eat himself to death if he didn't get to cook food for others at the diner.

I sighed and twisted my head to look out the window at the sound of tires crunching over gravel. My breath hitched at the sight of the beige Civic.

Gideon climbed from the car, then shoved the messy waves from his face. He glanced up, and I gasped. Instinct told me to duck under the window, but he squinted, and the brightness of the summer sun kept me concealed.

Footsteps distracted him. Grandpa Owl met Gideon in the gravel parking lot. In an exchange of shoulder pats and handshakes, my heart skipped a beat. Gideon was saying goodbye.

And he was the only one who knew about me.

Well, the only one who also wasn't a criminal, like Johnny and Bella.

"Are you sure you don't want to stay a little longer?" Grandpa Owl asked. I strained to catch their voices over the sound of the breeze rustling the leaves in Sherwood Forest.

"There's nothing left for me around here," Gideon said with a sigh. He shook his head and shoved his hands in his jeans pockets. "I didn't catch the thief, so my boss wants to let the case go cold. I'll be back on desk duty."

"I'm sorry to hear that," Grandpa Owl said.

"After the announcement this weekend, I'm gone," he said. "But I wish the best for Folklore Falls."

"It looks like you're leaving now." Grandpa Owl pointed to the duffle bag over Gideon's shoulder. The same bag that I'd rifled through when we first met. The memory twisted my stomach, and I swallowed a lump in my throat.

"I have to run back now to speak with my boss but I'll be back this weekend to wrap up the paperwork on this case."

After one more sturdy handshake between cop and seamster, Grandpa Owl sauntered back to the porch, where I heard Diana's voice call for him to come sit beside her. Apparently, he'd found company for the empty rocking chair next to his.

I smiled, but it didn't last. Gideon dropped back into the driver's seat, and my view of him vanished as he reversed and sped from the lot. A pang struck through my heart, and it suddenly felt real. I wouldn't see him again.

The vibration in my lap startled me. I yelped and snatched my phone up.

Bella: *Come out, come out wherever you are. Johnny has something for you from Officer Naughty, and it might be haunted. He left it on your porch.*

I rolled my eyes. Bella read too many gothic mysteries and contemporary romances. It combined with an odd effect of sounding like both a modern villain and a suspicious love interest.

Gideon will arrest me if he sees me.

I swiped away from the messages app and opened the video again. The unruly hair fell into his eyes as he fastened the handcuffs around Brett's wrists. Milan Jensen's voice screamed and cursed at Gideon from somewhere off the screen. The matriarch of the Jensen family had the most extreme reaction which signaled her guilt. Sure it was shame on her family name, but I never expected the carefully curated woman to allow herself to break down on live television.

The phone buzzed, and her text covered a quarter of the screen.

Bella: *You mean he'll put you in handcuffs? Sounds hot.*

I'm serious! I furiously tapped the screen, jabbing the letters with my fingers and huffing and puffing the whole time.

Bella: *Worth it. You've been moping for two weeks and so has he. Gideon walks around town like a stray dog. Something tells me he won't let you stay behind bars because he won't be able to hold you with the metal between you two.*

I turned the phone screen down on the floor and sighed. Maybe it was stupid to share with Bella what he'd said, but I was giddy, like a dumb teenager once again. She was a hopeless romantic, and it rubbed off on me.

With a groan, I picked up the phone again and typed an agreement.

Fine. I'll go to the reopening tonight to say goodbye to him.

Bella: *EEEEEK!*

Hearing yet another announcement from the Jensen family would make my stomach turn upside down. But it might be worth it to see Gideon one last time. I hopped to my feet, scrambled into my favorite green hoodie, and climbed out on the roof where I used the windows on the third, then second floors to scale down.

With the hood over my head, I blended into the green of Sherwood Forest and made my way through the trees.

When my house came into view, tears flooded my eyes. It didn't make sense. It was just a stupid, empty house, and I knew Betty was fine since Bella had been feeding her. But the forest, the sight of town and my neighborhood warmed me—I didn't belong hiding away in an attic.

Once I made it to the front steps, I hopped on the porch and paused.

A small brown bag tucked beside my welcome mat caught my eye. I stooped to pick up the bag made with the same burlap fabric I'd used to drop cash on people's doorsteps. Inside, silver reflected the sunlight. I pulled the note out first.

The message was short and simple, handwritten in all capitalized letters with blocky, clean font.

It isn't much, but it should help cover Billy's chemo and the cost of the bar exam for Sara. Gray area.

I plucked the silver chain and lifted the pocket watch from the bottom of the bag. The tears returned, burning my eyes. I chewed on my lip and closed my fist around the pocket watch.

Gideon not only listened to me, he remembered every word. What I cared about, he cared about.

And he still trusted me enough to do the right thing.

Which meant I had to do the *right thing*. The town gathering this weekend would provide the perfect opportunity to turn myself in.

GIDEON

The drive back to the city went by too quickly. One minute I could see Sherwood Bed and Breakfast in my rear view mirror, the next I pulled into the covered parking spot at my townhome. City smog hung over the street like a blanket of brown, but I didn't mind. The city suited me with its endless hustling. I appreciated the lack of dirt though it didn't stop me from tying my shoelaces together and suspending them on the hook inside my front door. I could hear Loxley's teasing inside my head until I refocused.

Everything looked normal, clean, and the same. This was the house I'd created for myself, my refuge after a tough day at the station—but today it felt different. Nothing had changed, and yet I felt displaced in a forgein life. Maybe I'd replace the simple furniture with antique pieces. I'd always loved old things but they didn't match with my lifestyle. As much as I appreciated the history behind them, I didn't have time for stories, or redecorating. I shook my head. Nothing needed to change, the plain space suited me just fine.

I headed for the small kitchen that stored nothing but protein meals and now-wilted spinach. Aside from the dust that had collected while I was gone, every surface remained pristine—wiped counters and spotless floors. After a bite of a protein bar, I crinkled the rest in the wrapper and tucked it inside the refrigerator. The faint chocolate flavor lingered on my tongue, and only served to make me crave the milkshake Loxley always ordered. Or maybe it was just the way her face lit up when she took a sip that I craved. A face I'd never see again. And it was just as well. I didn't need a reminder of the guilt that I'd let her go.

I swung the duffle bag over the back of the couch, and dropped it on the cushion.

I'd planned to relax when I arrived home, but the couch didn't look inviting. Instead, I rounded the corner to the bathroom and leaned over the sink. I sighed, and brushed my hair back. A shower would clear my head, so I reached for the collar at the back of my neck and pulled the shirt over my head.

Warm water pelted my chin and chest in a rhythmic, predictable splash. If I closed my eyes, the rush of water could have been the burst pipe. The reminder of Loxley springing into action made me smile. I'd admired her energy and determination before I knew she was a criminal.

I stepped into the stream and let the water pour over my face, but it did nothing to cleanse my memory. The slickness over my skin reminded me of climbing out of the falls and onto the slanted rock. I turned from the faucet and scrubbed the water away with a pass of my palm over my face.

Sunlight peeked through the slatted blinds over the small bathroom window—the only thing keeping the room from darkness. The stream of light through water looked nothing like the moonlight piercing through the falls from the backside, and yet I couldn't stop thinking about it.

I squeezed my eyes shut, and splashed a handful of water over my face. Showers were a ritual for me, a way to wash away the disappointment of dealing with crime everyday. But the water didn't cleanse me of guilt. The displaced feeling in my chest wasn't what I'd assumed.

I'd let Loxley go free, but the twist in my gut wasn't my conscience. Letting her go meant I would never see her again.

"Shoot," I breathed, and rested my palm on the wall behind the faucet. Even the mild curse reminded me of her. *I prefer loosing.* She was a spitfire, whip-smart but tempered. A liar. A thief. Good-hearted. Fascinating.

I pushed off the wall, and straightened. The lever squeaked as I turned off the faucet. I reached for a towel and scrubbed it over my face.

The face in the mirror didn't look like mine. I'd been frowning for so long, the scar from the accident molded into a nearly-permanent bend that only disappeared when I smiled. But I couldn't muster the energy.

Loxley had shattered my black and white beliefs. All I'd wanted to do when I fell for her was keep her safe, but she didn't need me.

I needed her.

"Time for a jog," I said to the man in the mirror. He looked pathetic, distracted, desperate to get his mind off of the liar.

Off of the truth.

I can't stop thinking about her.

Everything reminded me of the woman I'd met, and let go. I pulled gym shorts and a T-shirt on, and headed for the front door. The jog would kill time while I waited for the call from my boss to come into the precinct and go over the paperwork. But what about after? Would I bury myself in the desk again and forget a balance between work and life? The thought of returning to this house after my last trip to Folklore Falls this weekend sank my heart. My stomach felt heavy—all wrong for a jog.

But I had to clear my head.

I paused with my key in the door. Loxley always said goodbye to her pet fish, but I had no reason to hesitate. The townhome was empty, devoid of life, of color. It was merely a place to hang my clothes in between long hours at work.

I twisted the key until the lock clicked, and I turned to the side-walk. Instead of picking up my pace for a jog, I went straight for the covered parking.

My boss would have to deal with a discussion over the phone. We'd been communicating from a distance for weeks, anyway. Maybe she'd agree to a permanent relocation.

Loxley may never show her face to me again, and I couldn't blame her. We ran in different worlds. But I wanted to be in her's. So, I passed the precinct and kept on driving until the green hills of Folklore Falls came into view again.

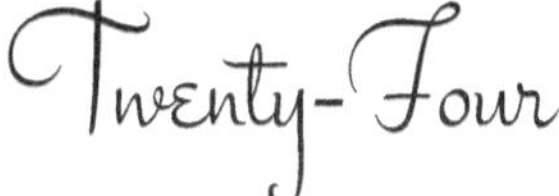

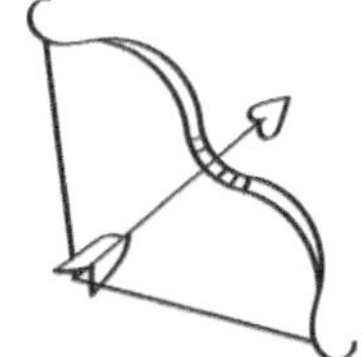

It was weird to see those I stole from mixed with my friends and family again. The last time, I hadn't noticed the discomfort of it because I'd been with Gideon. We'd walked into the Jensen Estate together, side-by-side, nearly hand-in-hand.

I squeezed my fist and approached the resort. At this gathering, the townsfolk wore their traditional flannels and jeans, which visually separated them from the elite in their luxury brand clothing. But Folklore Falls came together, vacationers and residents alike, for the real grand reopening. Everyone wanted to know the next surprise the Jensen family would spring on the town.

I already knew, of course, what Thomas Jensen would say after breaking into his study, and discovering his plan.

Mayor Richard took to the microphone again, this time on a large stage at the massive grounds of the resort behind a podium. The gates had been opened, inviting all inside for free on this one special occasion. Fountains decorated the garden that led to the event area. Three infinity pools dropped over the edge behind us, and the trellis had long been repaired.

The mayor welcomed Thomas Jensen to the stage for the second time in two weeks. Milan's arrest only brought them more fame and interest from the surrounding people. They'd quickly bought her way out of jail and donated a chunk of change to Folklore Falls State Park to save face.

"Nobody will have to worry about the dying town anymore," Thomas Jensen said, his voice echoing across the crowd. "We will provide a tour company, bakery, anything that you can want or imagine for Folklore Falls!"

Some cheers rose, mainly from the inebriated vacationers. Towns-folk exchanged worried looks.

"Exciting," Mayor Richard said, stepping up to the podium again. "You and your family have done so much good for Folklore Falls. We might need law enforcement around here who can see that." He chuckled.

I cringed and scanned the crowd for Gideon. His dark waves caught my eye. The frown on his face told me he hadn't missed the slight against him. Fire burned in my chest that fueled my energy, as I shoved my way to the front of the crowd.

The vacationers rewarded the mayor's joke with scattered laughter that inspired him to keep going.

"Perhaps the Jensens will hire private investigators to locate your stolen items," he said with an open palm pointed toward Thomas. Thomas nodded and smiled with a small wave at the audience.

I elbowed past Blondie and the Culps, who'd apparently decided they wanted to spend the entire summer in town. With an 'accidental' bump, I slipped the shining jewels from Blondie's bony wrist, and pressed into the crowd before she noticed it was missing.

The dark-haired cop stood with his arms crossed, and an expression so grumpy, it created a bubble around him. Though nobody stood too close to the angry man, the crowd still pulsed and pushed in around us with everybody clamoring for a glimpse of the overdecorated event area. I grabbed Gideon's wrist. He snapped his neck and froze at the sight of me. It could have been shock or trust, but he let me pull him toward me.

The press of bodies pushed me closer toward him. Though it was inappropriate, I longed to take the opportunity to taste his lips. Would he push me away?

Tense air hung between us. The scent of mint came with his every breath, and his jaw shifted.

Before I could give in to my baser desires, I blinked and refocused.

"Arrest me," I whispered.

His brows furrowed, and his dark eyes searched mine. I opened my palm and revealed the pearl bracelet from Blondie's wrist.

Gideon looked at my hand and swallowed.

"Arrest me and tell your boss you caught the thief," I said again, pressing closer to him. It wasn't meant to be selfish—I wanted him to handcuff me publicly before the mayor could make another joke at his expense. But if I was honest, I pushed against him so I could feel his body pressed on mine again. "I don't expect you to forgive me. I'm not asking for that. But I care about you, and this is the least I can do because… I love you." My eyes dropped for a moment, and I tilted my head with a small laugh. "Not to mention, I deserve it."

"My bracelet!" Blondie shrieked.

I nodded, my gaze holding his.

"Loxley Cameron, you're under arrest," he said. He spoke with determination in a low, hoarse voice. When I turned, he gently pulled my hands together behind my back and read me my rights. The cold metal on my skin was a stark contrast to his warm breath on my neck.

As wrong as it was in this moment, I couldn't help but think of Bella's words. It *was* hot for a second.

"You didn't have to do this," Gideon whispered into my ear. "I don't want to lock you up."

The thought of not seeing the falls again for a long time struck like lightning in my chest. But I'd thought this through. I'd survive and serve my time, and Gideon would keep his job where he could continue to protect people.

"Some things are black and white," I said. "And I'm a thief."

The crowd calmed when Gideon announced he'd caught me. He dropped the bracelet back in Blondie's hand and guided me through the bodies toward the exit. People parted to let us pass.

I closed my eyes as a familiar face came into view. Mama stood with Grandpa Owl and Diana at the edge of the crowd. Pain twisted her face, and it was like I was looking in a mirror of auburn hair wrapped in a claw.

When I opened my eyes, she wasn't looking at me. Diana whispered something to her and understanding dawned. It wasn't hard to put the threads together once they saw the guilt on my face. I stole, they received anonymous donations.

All eyes watched as Gideon directed me into the back seat of his car. I mouthed an apology to my family. I didn't want to hurt the people I loved the most anymore, even if it meant I'd be locked away from the falls.

And maybe I didn't spend decades carving a mountain for Gideon, but I did come clean.

GIDEON

The heat of the shower water turned my chest red. I'd hoped the beat of the water against my head would clear my thoughts and trigger an idea to get Loxley out. The bed-and-breakfast's water pressure was powerful, but didn't do the trick. Though I didn't miss my sterile townhome in the city. Once my boss had agreed to a relocation, I cut the lease. Eventually, I'd need to move out of Sherwood Bed and Breakfast, but not until I solved the case at hand.

Loxley was trapped.

And I'd promised her I would take her to the falls again soon, with a swear that I'd find a way to get her out. Yet here I was, in a warm shower while she sat in that uncomfortable cell.

I scrubbed shampoo through the tangles in my hair. Steam swirled around me even after the water shut off. I didn't have time for a haircut, so I wrapped it with a rubber band at the back of my head and threw on some clothes.

As I buttoned my pants, a knock rapped at the door. I kicked the duffle bag to the side and opened the door.

A dark-haired woman smiled at me. She held her toddler on one hip and extended her hand for a shake.

"You don't know me," she said, "But I'm Sara Ellery, and this is my son, Grayson."

"After the legend?" I asked. Loxley had piqued my interest with her passion, and I'd read up on it after our visit to the caves.

Sara smiled. "I've taken and passed the bar thanks to Loxley's—" she cleared her throat, "donations. As a practicing lawyer, I'd like to represent her case, and I was told you were the one who might be interested in helping me gather the evidence to get her released."

I nodded. "Yes, will you come in?" I moved from the doorway and invited her inside.

"Unfortunately, I have somewhere to be," she said. "Hopping between places and all." The toddler raised his hand to wave at me as she hefted him higher on her hip. The boy held a small burlap bag in his wrist, one of the same kind Loxley would use to spread her donations. He extended his arm and held it out until I took it.

"You'll find that it's enough to post her bail," Sara said.

I uncurled the check that had been rolled and tucked into the bag.

"Was this money come by legally?" I asked. "Two wrongs..." I said it, but I couldn't admit I meant it. The gray area had become my home. Black and white rules couldn't cover everything, and I knew that now. After promising her she'd see the falls again, I nearly slipped into the station in the dark to let her out for a hike and a swim. But I couldn't risk digging her deeper into trouble, so I'd resisted.

Sara nodded. "The people Loxley helped have pooled change together. The whole town. It should be enough to get her out while we build a case to clear her name."

"I don't trust people easily," I admitted. "I don't know if I can take this without proof of the source after everything."

The boy's freckles and red hair matched his inquisitive expression. I tried to hand them the check, but Sara stepped back.

"I can't lie," she said.

I snorted. "Like George Washington?"

Sara didn't appreciate the joke, but the boy smiled.

"I'm sorry," I said. "Your son looks so familiar. Are you sure we haven't met?"

"He gets that a lot," she said. "His father is well known around here. Oh, and I've got a case against the Jensens as well. Thanks to Loxley's help with my schooling plus the information she gathered on the family, I'm able to finally approach this. The Jensens built their resort on illegal land, and I intend to expose this. It was never zoned for commercial use. Technically, that is all historic land. If you're interested in digging into this case with me, I'll be back in this…" Ms. Ellery paused and looked around. "This area soon. Keep in touch."

I nodded and lifted the check. "Okay, thank you. If you'll excuse me, I'd like to get Loxley out as soon as possible."

"I'll see you in court," she said.

Sara didn't seem to mind my rushed attitude. By the time I pulled my shoes off the hooks and shoved my feet into them, she'd disappeared from the hallway. I marched to the car, nearly picking my feet up in a run. I wasn't proud to say I'd broken the speed limit on the drive to the bail bondsman's office. The two hours it took to process the paperwork drove me mad. I almost lost it when they said it could take the rest of the day.

I grabbed the unfinished paperwork, and the receptionist yelled after me.

Once inside the station, Sheriff Max greeted me from behind the desk with a mouthful of Fryer Tuck's burger to-go. I nodded and grunted a hello, then threw the paperwork on his desk.

"Bail is posted," I said.

Sheriff Max sat up, and his chair squeaked from the shifted weight.

"This paperwork ain't finished," he said.

"I don't care." I shook my head and grabbed the keys. It amazed me they still used the old-fashioned lock system rather than digitizing it.

Loxley huddled in the cell's corner with her arms wrapped around her. She looked up when I approached.

"Hey," she said. "What's going on?"

"I'm taking you to the falls like I promised."

Loxley stood and reached her arm through the bars. I jiggled the old key in the lock, but it was stuck, which required me to pull it out and insert again.

Her hand covered mine. "Don't get us both in trouble."

"This is perfectly legal," I said, shoving the key in the lock again. With a jiggle, it turned and released the lever. I yanked the cell door open and pulled her toward me. "But what we're about to do next is a gray area."

Loxley tilted her head, but her smile revealed she trusted me. With my fingers intertwined with hers, I pulled her toward the storage room.

"I haven't organized—" Sheriff Max started.

Evidence tags marked items. Other objects were nothing more than lost and found from around the town. I grabbed the bag with the dagger. The diamond blade caught the dim station's light and sent reflections in every direction.

"This belongs to the state park," I said, lifting the bag above my head. Loxley's smile delighted me. The sheriff didn't stop us, so I directed Loxley outside and opened the door to my car.

"I hear the hike is a tough one," I said.

Loxley laughed and nodded. "Do we need fuel?"

I plopped into the driver's seat. "And comfortable clothes."

LOXLEY

The clothes we'd stopped and changed into didn't matter. Summer had arrived in full force, and by the time we'd climb to the falls, we both dripped with sweat. The evening didn't bring a breeze, but with the sun dipping behind the horizon, we'd get relief soon.

It took some peer pressure, but Gideon agreed to strip down to his underwear with me to make the swim easier. His reservations kept me from behaving too recklessly. Without him, I might have gone full nude to get out of the sweaty bra, which could get me in a lot of trouble if anybody hiked out here and saw me.

The falls crashed and sprayed a constant mist at us as we lifted ourselves onto the slab of rock behind the water. He left his legs dangling in the water while I swung one of mine over the other side of him. The salty, minty taste of him sent a rush of heat through my veins.

Gideon's grip on my hips elicited a moan from me, and we pressed our wet bodies against one another.

"I still don't think I deserve your forgiveness," I said, wiping the wet waves from his forehead.

"You can make it up to me," he said with a smile that made his scar disappear.

"Yeah? How do I do that?"

Gideon lifted me off him and stood. He offered to help me up, then grabbed me by the shoulders. The moment felt like one I'd already lived except the roles were flipped. He moved me into the where I could see the outcropping of rocks where Oberon and Titiana supposedly once sat and witnessed Grayson Baird and Ellery's wedding.

"I didn't understand you," he said. "And it fascinated me. Then, when I learned who you really were, what fascinated me was that I didn't hate you. Not even a little. I wondered how I could be drawn to someone so corrupt until I realized you had a good heart. But I can't say I agree with how you did things—stealing and lying."

"Okay, okay," I said, putting my finger to his mouth. "I know I was wrong, and I want to make it up to you."

Gideon raked his fingers through his hair and scrubbed the back of his neck with his palm. "Look, I know this is going to sound crazy because we've only known each other for a short time."

The thumping in my heart picked up again after having calmed when I caught my breath. I tilted my head to catch Gideon's gaze but he kept it firmly on the water rippling beneath the rock.

"It's just that I've lost someone I cared about before and I don't want to waste a second of time with you." He finally looked up at my hands, and absently traced the scars from botched break-ins and over my knuckles. The fall from the trellis at Jensen Resort left my wrist with a small jagged gash that his fingertips found. He met my gaze and took a deep breath. "I know how quickly that can be taken away."

"What are you saying?" I could read him, his nerves were as plain as a sentence in a book. The way he spoke, rushing everything and using clipped sentences could have been the title of a novel, or a poem. Everything about it said Gideon, but a nervous Gideon.

"Isn't this where the faery stood?" he asked. The sudden change in the subject startled me. I raised my eyebrows and looked at my feet to confirm where I stood. He'd moved us into the same position where we'd shared our first kiss.

"That's the legend," I said with a shrug. My casual demeanor vanished when Gideon dropped to one knee. Breath left my lungs, and my voice fell to a whisper. "Fox in a henhouse."

"You could say yes," he said. "I mean, you don't have to marry me to make it up to me. I already forgive you, and I love you. I just thought it was a good segue, and now that I hear it—"

"You're terrible with words." I laughed. "But you said you love me."

"I do," he said, as if this were the wedding itself. All the nerves dissipated and he held my gaze. "Uh, but I don't have a ring."

I pulled the hair claw from the back of my head and let the wet hair fall over my shoulders. "You can clip this on my finger."

"Weird idea," he said.

"I have a lot of those."

Gideon opened his mouth to ask what I couldn't wait to hear, but I stopped him.

"Are you sure you want to marry someone with a criminal past?" I asked.

"You're more than just one thing," he said. "Loxley Cameron, will you marry me?"

I tried to speak, but my voice left me. My throat tightened, and I nodded, allowing tears to fill my eyes. With my hand still holding his, I tugged him to stand and wrapped my arms around his neck.

We kissed behind Folklore Falls, letting the watery mist wash away the mistakes from our past.

<h1 style="text-align:center">Epilogue</h1>

2 YEARS AND 9 MONTHS LATER

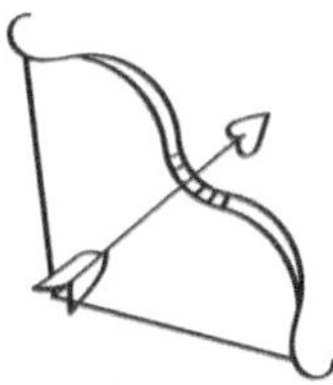

The bell on the front door jingled. I pulled the ring off my finger and secured it in a small burlap bag, then tucked it into my pocket. Movement made my limbs swell these days, and today would require a lot of time on my feet.

The diamond blade in the center of the room sent glowing spots over the walls and ceilings. The old bakery reinvented to a small museum with a lot of clean-up and a little love.

Glass cases that once held Diana's delicious homemade bread and cinnamon streusel cake now displayed pieces of Folklore Falls's history.

I smiled at the couple who came through the door. "I'm sorry," I said, resting my hand on my stomach. "We're not available to the public yet. Tonight is our grand opening event. If you come back at seven, Baird's Historical Gallery will invite everyone in for free for this evening only."

"Oh," the woman said. "We have reservations with a tour guide for the waterfalls tonight. What will you charge for entry tomorrow?"

"Ten dollars," I said, struggling to take a deep breath. "But the money goes directly into helping the town's residents and preserving the history of Folklore Falls."

The woman nodded and smiled. "Thank you, and congratulations." She pointed to my stomach.

"Are you stealing basketballs and swallowing them?" a deep voice behind me said. Gideon wrapped his arms around my waist and pulled me against him.

"Just what every pregnant woman wants to hear," I said. "Someday, I'll teach you how to give real compliments."

"Hmm," he hummed. His lips brushed my neck, then behind my ear. Shivers trickled up my spine and beneath my hair. I turned and took his face in my hands. We kissed until the bell chimed again.

Bella approached with her hands on her hips and a haughty smile. "Great," she said. "You've gone from a grumpy, scary-looking cop to a grumpy, scary-looking security guard at the world's tiniest museum."

"I'm still working cases for Sheriff Max," Gideon said, defending himself.

I rolled my eyes at the constant hostility between my best friend and my husband. It would have happened no matter who I married. Bella was hostile to everyone's boyfriends or husbands because they weren't the perfect tortured men from gothic romances. She believed jokes at others' expense were a love language. It was all bark, though. She'd cried when Gideon read his vows to me. That was the only lie I still told since she demanded it under threat of death by book beating.

"You mean you're doing Max's job while he naps in his car?" I asked. "And we know you have an obsession with oversized things, but it doesn't mean you have to knock Baird's Gallery."

Purple lips spread into a smile. She'd shifted her style to all purple now, the color of royalty.

"Speaking of oversized jerkwads," she said, "Brett the Bully is supposed to be coming back into town for the official sale of the Jensen Estate." The memory of the Jensens backing out of the campaign for mayor made me frown. After the resort's exposed destruction of a historical place had smeared their 'good' name, Thomas withdrew. They'd gotten what they deserved, but it didn't come without plenty of suffering from Folklore Falls residents first. At least I could put a life of crime behind me now that I'd found another way to funnel funds to locals. And with Grandpa Owl as Mayor, I could breathe easier that Sherwood Forest and the falls would stay intact.

"What are you thinking?" I asked, grabbing a dust rag and swiping it over the display cases. Gideon walked the aisles again, triple-checking the width with a measuring tape to be sure wheelchairs and strollers would fit with ease.

"I think I'm going to pay him a visit," she said. "Plus, that mansion has been empty for months. If it's haunted, I want to be the first to witness the ghosts."

"Wouldn't that mean Brett would witness it first?" I asked. I licked my thumb and scrubbed off a smudge on the glass of the dagger's case.

"Exactly." she lowered her voice. "So, I want to get there first."

I arched my eyebrow and turned to her.

"One last break-in?" she asked.

Gideon was out of earshot. He tested the cash register for the hundredth time to be sure everything worked before the opening tonight. His fixation on rules had relaxed but had manifested later into mild perfectionism with all things museum-related.

"What would you do if I broke the law?" I asked, shouting across the museum. Bella straightened and swatted my arm. She shushed me, but she knew I kept no secrets from him.

Gideon didn't look up or miss a beat. "Handcuff you to our bed."

"Promise?"

My husband smirked, shook his head, then met my gaze over the artifacts and display cases. The building was crisp, clean, and cold. But one look from Gideon, and my entire body warmed. I could taste him whenever I wanted, but I didn't have the patience to wait to be in his arms until after Bella left. To avoid being rude to my best friend, when I made my way across the gallery, I only hugged him.

Gideon's breath tickled my ear as he whispered. "I'm looking forward to it."

THANK YOU FOR READING!

PLEASE CONSIDER LEAVING A REVIEW AT YOUR FAVORITE PLACE TO PURCHASE BOOKS IF YOU ENJOYED THIS STORY! ALSO, A SHARE WITH YOUR FRIENDS WHO LOVE CLEAN, SWEET, SMALL-TOWN ROMANCES WOULD BE GREATLY APPRECIATED. MY QUEST AS AN AUTHOR IS TO MAKE OTHERS FEEL SEEN THROUGH THE ADVENTURE OF FICTION. PLEASE REACH OUT TO ME AND LET ME KNOW IF MY STORIES HAVE TOUCHED YOU. YOU, DEAR READER, ARE WHO THIS BOOK WAS WRITTEN FOR.

About the Author

Congenital Heart Defect survivor, Emily Fluke, finds joy and peace through the expression of writing. She is a firm believer that all stories need a little magic and a lot of excitement. Emily and her husband spend their free time wrangling two children and playing video games in their busy California lifestyle. Otherwise, you'll find Emily solving an escape room, running, or writing Magic the Gathering-based poetry.

To stay up to date on new releases and connect with me, visit my website at Emilyfluke.com or follow me on social media under Author Emily Fluke, or @emilyflukefairytales

Special Preview

I can't wait to share another escape into the idyllic town of Folklore Falls with you! Join me in celebrating the happily ever after retelling of a certain beauty and a notorious beast. Read on for a special preview of Fake Dating's a Beast.

FAKE DATING'S A BEAST RELEASES ON OCTOBER 11TH, 2022.

Fake Dating's a Beast Excerpt

Nobody was allowed to see me cry, which meant I had to read *Phantom of the Opera* in the solitary confinement of the book-store's storage room. Gaston Leroux broke my heart when he killed Erik, and that still didn't compare to Christine's choice of eloping with Raoul. The jerk promised to take her away from the Opera House, even if she didn't want it. Who runs away to marry a guy that basically threatened to kidnap her?

Besides me, of course. But I'd only do that if the man was fictional. Alas, my life wasn't a novel, and Folklore Falls didn't offer storybook romances with dark and brooding men.

Not unless you were my best friend. Loxley and Gideon were about to pop out their first baby after a whirlwind romance, then a year of engagement and another year married. I'd picked up a few trade secrets on the lying front, and claimed my only tearful breakdown was at their precious wedding.

And I cried. Sure. But it wasn't because of the *beauty* of it all—I wasn't that sappy. I cried because of the curse.

A muffled jingle snapped my attention to the present. The bell on the bookstore's front door chimed, so I slapped the pages of the gothic novel shut and hopped off the stool. I slipped between the maze of stacked books in the storage room and emerged to see a familiar face.

"Speak of the devil," I muttered.

Officer Notting knocked into a stack of precariously balanced bodice-rippers, and the tower toppled into a pile of novels. I rolled my eyes, but he didn't so much as apologize. The wild look in Gideon's eyes told me he didn't have the headspace to worry about the mess he'd just created in my shop.

"Loxley is in labor," he said, raking his hand through his hair. Sweat shined on his forehead like a beacon of desperation. "She won't let me take her to the hospital. You're the only one she listens to when she gets stubborn like this."

"Fine," I said, as I marched past him and pushed through the door.

"Thank you."

I only shrugged and doubled back to grab one of my favorite bodice-rippers. The worn pages felt like a home I could hold in my hand. I snuck a sniff of the well-loved book before tucking it under my arm.

"What do you need a book for?"

"Labor is longer than you think," I said.

"We're taking her to the hospital. Now." Gideon jabbed his finger at his feet as if his sheer determination could save the day.

"We'll see," I said. "Good thing I've read plenty of romances with midwives."

"You're going to convince her, right?"

I shrugged again, my signature move meaning *whatever*.

"Right?" His voice pitched higher in desperation.

"And I'll meet a tall, dark doctor and fall madly in love," I said. I spun around and twisted the key in the bookstore's lock.

"Shoot," he cursed. "What in the world are you talking about?"

A coming autumn breeze tossed my hair into my face. I plucked the dyed strands of black from sticking to my lipstick and ruining the perfect shade of purple. Folklore Falls' trees had turned red and brown. Leaves covered the parking lot and orange pumpkins lined the front of the shops in town.

"The curse," I mumbled, "I'm talking about the curse of single-hood. Not that you'd know anything about it."